Praise for Alice Adams and
THE LAST LOVELY CITY

"The stories in *The Last Lovely City* present engaging, realistic and modern perspectives on mature relationships. Adams invites us into a fictional world remarkably untouched by our culture's obsessive concern with youth and the romantic struggles of twentysomethings."

—*Ft. Lauderdale Sun-Sentinel*

"Adams is, like Colette, a consummate, sly, wise, quick-witted sketch artist. . . . Her connections are made with every nerve bristlingly alive."

—*The Oxford American*

"Adams has a gift for fluid, unlabored prose. She distills life's ordinary triumphs and disappointments into smooth paragraphs that have more punch than their quiet tone seems to promise."

—*e Times*

"Highly crafted and w

xican

"Enjoy these stories and then run out and pick up one of Alice Adams' longer works which you may not yet have had the good fortune to have read."

—*Des Moines Register*

Medicine Men

"A painful and hilarious sendup of grandiose doctors and their barbaric medical miracles. . . . A postmodern Jane Austen romp."

—*Boston Globe*

Second Chances

"An ambitious, wise, brilliantly executed novel. . . . Alice Adams belongs in the company of a very small group of contemporary novelists who seem to know everything worth knowing about human beings."

—*Cleveland Plain Dealer*

Superior Women

"Reads easily, even breathlessly . . . the subtle but intensely felt shifts of closeness among the young women are lovingly and expertly laid bare."

—John Updike

Available from Washington Square Press

THE LAST LOVELY CITY

STORIES BY

ALICE ADAMS

WASHINGTON SQUARE PRESS
PUBLISHED BY POCKET BOOKS

New York   London   Toronto   Sydney   Singapore

WSP

A Washington Square Press Publication of
POCKET BOOKS, a division of Simon & Schuster Inc.
1230 Avenue of the Americas, New York, NY 10020

Published by arrangement with Alfred A. Knopf, Inc.

Some of these stories originally appeared in the following publications:

"The Haunted Beach," *Boulevard;* "Patients" and "The Wrong Mexico," *Cross Currents;* "His Women," "Old Love Affairs," "The Last Lovely City," "The Drinking Club," and "Earthquake Damage," *The New Yorker;* "The Islands," *Ontario Review;* "The Visit," *Ploughshares;* "Great Sex" and "A Very Nice Dog," *Southwest Review*

ISBN: 0-671-03618-1

First Washington Square Press trade paperback printing February 2000

10 9 8 7 6 5 4 3 2 1

WASHINGTON SQUARE PRESS and colophon are registered trademarks of Simon & Schuster Inc.

Cover design by Brigid Pearson; front cover photo by Ellis Herwig/Stock Boston/PNI

Printed in the U.S.A.

To
Peter Adams Linenthal
and Philip Anasovich
with much love

Contents

PART ONE

His Women

"I think we should try it again. You move back in," says Meredith, in her lovely, low, dishonest Southern voice.

Carter asks, "But—Adam?"

"I'm not seeing him anymore." Her large face, not pretty but memorable, braves his look of disbelief. Her big, deep-brown eyes are set just too close; her shapely mouth is a little too full, and greedy. Big, tall, dark, sexy Meredith, who is still by law his wife. She adds, "I do see him around the campus, I mean, but we're just friends now."

That's what you said before, Carter does not say, but that unspoken sentence hangs there in the empty space between them. She knows it as well as he does.

They are sitting in the garden behind her house—their house, actually, joint ownership being one of their central problems, as Carter sees it. In any case, now in early summer, in Chapel Hill, the garden is lovely. The roses over which Carter has labored in seasons past—pruning, spraying, and carefully, scientifically feeding—are in fragrant, delicately full bloom: great bursts of red and flame, yellow and pink and white. The beds are untidy now, neglected. Adam, who never actually moved in (Carter thinks), is not a gardener, and Meredith has grown careless.

She says, with a pretty laugh, "We're not getting younger. Isn't it time we did something mature, like making our marriage work?"

"Since we can't afford a divorce." He, too, laughs, but since what he says is true, no joke, it falls flat.

And Meredith chooses to ignore it; they are not to talk about money, not this time. "You know I've always loved you," she says, her eyes larger and a warmer brown than ever.

Perhaps in a way she has, thinks Carter. Meredith loves everyone; it is a part of her charm. Why not him, too? Carter and Adam and all her many friends and students (Meredith teaches in the music department at the university), and most cats and dogs and birds.

She adds, almost whispering, sexily, "And I think you love me, too. We belong together."

"I'll have to think about it," Carter tells her, somewhat stiffly.

The brown eyes narrow, just a little. "How about Chase? You still see her?"

"Well, sort of." He does not say "as friends," since this is not true, though Carter has understood that the presence of Chase in his life has raised his stature—his value, so to speak—and he wishes he could say that they are still "close."

But four years of military school, at The Citadel, left Carter a stickler for the literal truth, along with giving him his ramrod posture and a few other unhelpful hangups—according to the shrink he drives over to Durham to see, twice a week. Dr. Chen, a diminutive Chinese of mandarin manners and a posture almost as stiff in its way as Carter's own. ("Oh, great," was Chase's comment on hearing this description. "You must think you're back in some Oriental Citadel.") In any case, he is unable to lie now to Meredith, who says, with a small and satisfied laugh, "So we're both free. It's fated, you see?"

A long time ago, before Meredith and long before Chase, Carter was married to Isabel, who was small and fair and thin and rich, truly beautiful and chronically unfaithful. In those days, Carter was a graduate student at the university, in business administration, which these days he teaches. They lived, back then, he and Isabel, in a fairly modest rented house out on Franklin Street, somewhat crowded with Isabel's valuable inherited antiques; the effect was grander than that of any other graduate students', or even young professors', homes. As Isabel was grander, more elegant than other wives, in her big hats and long skirts and very high heels, with her fancy hors d'oeuvres and her collection of forties big-band tapes, to which she loved to dance. After dinner, at parties at their house, as others cleared off the table, Isabel would turn up the music and lower the lights in the living room. "Come *on,*" she would say. "Let's all *dance.*"

Sometimes there were arguments later:

"I feel rather foolish saying this, but I don't exactly like the way you dance with Walter."

"Whatever do you mean? Walter's a marvelous dancer." But she laughed unpleasantly, her wide, thin, dark-red mouth showing small, perfect teeth; she knew exactly what he meant.

What do you do if your wife persists in dancing *like that* in your presence? And if she even tells you, on a Sunday, that she thinks she will drive to the beach with Sam, since you have so many papers to grade?

She promises they won't be late, and kisses Carter good-bye very tenderly. But they are late, very late. Lovely Isabel, who comes into the house by herself and is not only late but a little drunk, as Carter himself is by then, having had considerable bourbon for dinner, with some peanuts for nourishment.

Nothing that he learned at The Citadel had prepared Carter for any of this.

Standing in the doorway, Isabel thrusts her body into a dancer's pose, one thin hip pushed forward and her chin, too, stuck out—a sort of mime of defiance. She says, "Well, what can I say? I know I'm late, and we drank too much."

"Obviously."

"But so have you, from the look of things."

"I guess."

"Well, let's have another drink together. What the hell. We always have fun drinking, don't we, darling Carter?"

"I guess."

It was true. Often, drinking, they had hours of long, wonderful, excited conversations, impossible to recall the following day. As was the case this time, the night of Isabel's Sunday at the beach with Sam.

Drinking was what they did best together; making love was not. This was something they never discussed, although back then, in the early seventies, people did talk about it quite a lot, and many people seemed to do it all the time. But part of their problem, sexually, had to do with drink itself, not surprisingly. A few belts of bourbon or a couple of Sunday-lunch martinis made Isabel aggressively amorous, full of tricks and wiles and somewhat startling perverse persuasions. But Carter, although his mind was aroused and his imagination inflamed, often found himself incapacitated. Out of it, turned off. This did not always happen, but it happened far too often.

Sometimes, though, there were long, luxurious Sunday couplings, perhaps with some breakfast champagne or some dope; Isabel was extremely fond of an early-morning joint. Then it could be as great as any of Carter's boyhood imaginings of sex.

But much more often, as Isabel made all the passionate gestures in her considerable repertoire, Carter would have to murmur, "Sorry, dear," to her ear. Nuzzling, kissing her neck. "Sorry I'm such a poop."

And so it went the night she came home from Sam, from the beach. They had some drinks, and they talked. "Sam's actually kind of a jerk," said Isabel. "And you know, we didn't actually do anything. So let's go to bed. Come, kiss me and say I'm forgiven, show me I'm forgiven." But he couldn't show her, and at last it was she who had to forgive.

Another, somewhat lesser problem was that Isabel really did not like Chapel Hill. "It's awfully pretty," she admitted, "and we do get an occasional good concert, or even an art show. But, otherwise, what a terrifically overrated town! And the faculty wives, now really. I miss my friends."

Therefore Carter was pleased, he was very pleased, when Isabel began to speak with some warmth of this new friend, Meredith. "She's big and fat, in fact she's built like a cow, and she's very Southern, but she has a pretty voice and she works in the music department, she teaches there, and she seems to have a sense of humor. You won't mind if I ask her over?"

Meeting Meredith, and gradually spending some time with her, Carter at first thought she was a good scout, like someone's sister. Like many big women (Isabel's description had been unkind), she had a pleasant disposition and lovely skin. Nice long brown hair, and her eyes, if just too closely placed, were the clear, warm brown of Southern brooks. With Carter, her new friend's husband, she was flirty in a friendly, pleasant way—the way of Southern women, a way he was used to. She was like his mother's friends, and his cousins, and the nice girls from Ashley Hall whom he used to take to dances at The Citadel.

Meredith became the family friend. She was often invited to dinner parties, or sometimes just for supper by herself. She and Isabel always seemed to have a lot to talk about. Concerts in New York, composers and musicians, not to mention a lot of local gossip.

When they were alone, Carter gathered, they talked about Meredith's boyfriends, of which she seemed to have a large and steady supply. "She's this certain type of Southern belle," was

Isabel's opinion. "Not threateningly attractive, but sexy and basically comfy. She makes men feel good, with those big adoring cow eyes."

Did Isabel confide in Meredith? Carter suspected that she did, and later he found out for certain from Meredith that she had. About her own affairs. Her boyfriends.

Although he had every reason to know that she was unhappy, Carter was devastated by Isabel's departure. Against all reason, miserably, he felt that his life was demolished. Irrationally, instead of remembering a bitter, complaining Isabel ("I can't stand this tacky town a minute longer") or an Isabel with whom things did not work out well in bed ("Well, Jesus Christ, is that what you learned at The Citadel?"), he recalled only her beauty. Her clothes, and her scents. Her long blond hair.

He was quite surprised, at first, when Meredith began to call a lot with messages of sympathy, when she seemed to take his side. "You poor guy, you certainly didn't deserve this," was one of the things she said at the time. Told that he was finding it hard to eat—"I don't know, everything I try tastes awful"—she began to arrive every day or so, at mealtimes, with delicately flavored chicken and oven-fresh Sally Lunn, tomatoes from her garden, and cookies, lots and lots of homemade cookies. Then she took to inviting him to her house for dinner—often.

As he left her house, at night, Carter would always kiss Meredith, in a friendly way, but somehow, imperceptibly, the kisses and their accompanying embraces became more prolonged. Also, Carter found that this good-night moment was something he looked forward to. Until the night when Meredith whispered to him, "You really don't have to go home, you know. You could stay with me." More kissing, and then, "Please stay. I want you, my darling Carter."

Sex with Meredith was sweet and pleasant and friendly, and

if it lacked the wild rush that he had sometimes felt with Isabel, at least when he failed her she was nice about it. Sweet and comforting. Unlike angry Isabel.

They married as soon as his divorce was final, and together they bought the bargain house, on a hill outside town, and they set about remodeling: shingling, making a garden, making a kitchen and a bedroom with wonderful views. Carter, like everyone else in the high-flying eighties, had made some money on the market, and he put all this into the house. The house became very beautiful; they loved it, and in that house Carter and Meredith thrived. Or so he thought.

He thought so until the day she came to him in anguished tears and told him, "This terrible thing. I've fallen in love with Adam." Adam, a lean young musician, a cellist, who had been to the house for dinner a couple of times. Unprepossessing, Carter would have said.

Carter felt, at first, a virile rage. Bloodily murderous fantasies obsessed his waking hours; at night he could barely sleep. He was almost unrecognizable to himself, this furiously, righteously impassioned man. With Meredith he was icily, enragedly cold. And then, one day, Meredith came to him and with more tears she told him, "It's over, I'll never see him again. Or if I do we'll just be friends."

After that followed a brief and intense and, to Carter, slightly unreal period of, well, fucking: the fury with which they went at each other could not be called "making love." Meredith was the first to taper off; she responded less and less actively, although as always she was pleasant, nice. But Carter finally asked her what was wrong, and she admitted, through more tears, "It's Adam. I'm seeing him again. I mean, we're in love again."

This time, Carter reacted not with rage but with a sort of defeated grief. He felt terribly old and battered. *Cuckold.*

The ugly, old-fashioned word resounded, echoing through his brain. He thought, I am the sort of man to whom women are unfaithful.

When he moved out, away from Meredith and into an apartment, and Chase Landau fell in love with him (quite rapidly, it seemed), Carter assumed that she must be crazy. It even seemed a little nuts for her to ask him for dinner soon after they met, introducing themselves in the elevator. Chase lived in his building, but her apartment, which contained her studio, was about twice the size of Carter's and much nicer, with balconies and views. "I liked your face," she later explained. "I always go for those narrow, cold, mean eyes." Laughing, making it a joke.

Chase was a tall, thin, red-haired woman, not Southern but from New York, and somewhat abrasive in manner. A painter of considerable talent and reputation (no wonder Meredith was impressed). Carter himself was impressed at finding inquiries from *Who's Who* lying around, especially because she never mentioned it. In his field, only the really major players made it.

Her paintings were huge, dark, and violent abstractions, incomprehensible. Discomforting. How could anyone buy these things and live with them? As they sat having drinks that first night, working at light conversation, Carter felt the paintings as enormous, hostile presences.

Chase was almost as tall as Carter, close to six feet, and thin, but heavy-breasted, which may have accounted for her bad posture; she tended to slouch, and later she admitted, "When I was very young I didn't like my body at all. So conspicuous." Carter liked her body, very much. Her eyes were intense and serious, always.

As they were finishing dinner she said to him, "Your shoulders are wonderful. I mean the angle of them. This," and she reached with strong hands to show him.

He found himself aroused by that touch, wanting to turn

and grasp her. To kiss. But not doing so. Later on, he did kiss her good night, but very chastely.

Used to living with women, with Isabel and then with Meredith, Carter began to wonder what to do by himself at night. He had never been much of a reader, and most television bored him. In the small town that Chapel Hill still was in many ways, you would think (Carter thought) that people knowing of the separation would call and ask him over, but so far no one had. He wished he had more friends; he should have been warmer, kinder. Closer to people. He felt very old, and alone. (He wondered, *Are* my eyes mean? Am *I* mean?)

He called Chase and asked her out to dinner. "I know it's terribly short notice, but are you busy tonight?"

"No, in fact I'd love to go out tonight. I'm glad you called."

His heart leaped up at those mild words.

During that dinner, Chase talked quite a lot about the art world: her New York gallery, the one in L.A., the local art department. He listened, grateful for the entertainment she provided, but he really wasn't paying much attention. He was thinking of later on: would she, possibly, so soon—

She would not. At the door, she bid him a clear good night after a rather perfunctory social kiss. She thanked him for the dinner. She had talked too much, she feared; she tended to do that with new people, she told him, with a small, not quite apologetic, laugh.

From a friend in the law school, Carter got the name of a lawyer, a woman, with whom he spent an uncomfortable, discouraging, and expensive half hour. What it came to was that in order to recover his share in the house, Carter would have to force Meredith to sell it, unless she could buy him out. None of this was final, of course; it was just the lawyer's temporary take on things. Still, it was deeply depressing to Carter.

Coming home, in the downstairs lobby of his building he ran into Chase, who was carrying a sack of groceries, which of course he offered to take.

"Only if you'll come and have supper with me." She flashed him a challenging smile. "I must have been thinking of you. I know I bought too much."

That night it was he who talked a lot. She only interrupted from time to time with small but sharp-edged questions. "If you didn't want to go to The Citadel, why didn't you speak up?" And, "Do you think you trusted Meredith at first because she's not as good-looking as Isabel?" The sort of questions that he usually hated—that he hated from Dr. Chen—but not so with Chase; her dark, intelligent eyes were kind and alert. He almost forgot his wish to make love to her.

But then he remembered, and all that desire returned. He told her, "It's all I can do not to touch you. You're most terrifically attractive to me."

By way of answer, she smiled and leaned to meet him in a kiss. For a long time, then, like adolescents, they sat there kissing on her sofa, until she whispered, "Come on, let's go to bed. This is silly."

Carter had not expected their progress to be quite so rapid. He hardly knew her; did he really want this? But not long after that, they were indeed in bed, both naked. He caressed her soft, heavy breasts.

Pausing, sitting up to reach somewhere, Chase said, "You'll have to wear this. I'm sorry."

"Oh, Lord. I haven't done that since I was twenty. And look, I'm safe. I never played around."

"I know, but Meredith did. A lot."

"I don't think I can—"

"Here, I'll help you."

"Damn, I'm losing it; I knew I would."

Strictly speaking, technically, that night was not a great success. Still, literally they had gone to bed together, and Carter's feeling was that this was not a woman who fell into bed very easily (unlike—he had to think this—either Isabel or Meredith).

The next day he had another appointment with the lawyer, who had talked with Meredith's lawyer, who had said that things looked worse.

"I don't know why I'm so drawn to you," Chase told him, "but I really am." She laughed. "That's probably not a good sign. For you, I mean. The men I've really liked best were close to certifiable. But you're not crazy, are you?"

"Not so far as I know."

Chase did not seem crazy to him. She was hardworking, very intelligent. Her two sons, with whom she got along well, were off in school, and she was surrounded by warm and admiring friends; her phone rang all the time with invitations, friendly voices. But, as Carter put it to himself, she did sometimes seem a little much. A little more than he had bargained for. Or more than he was up to right now.

Their sexual life, despite her continued insistence on—hated phrase—"safe sex," was sometimes great, then not. Chase complained, though nicely, that out of bed he was not affectionate. "I could use more plain, unsexy touching," she said, and he tried to comply, though demonstrativeness was not at all in his nature.

Carter's broker called with bad news, quite a lot of bad news. Carter, like most people in the market, had taken a beating.

Even Chase would admit that her work habits were a little strange. She liked to get up late and spend a couple of hours drinking coffee, phoning, maybe writing a letter or two. She would then go into her studio (a room to which Carter was never admitted). At times she would emerge to eat a piece of fruit, heat some soup, or, less frequently, go out for a short walk along the graveled paths of old Chapel Hill. Back in her studio, immersed in her work, quite often she would forget about dinner until ten at night, or eleven; she did not forget dinner dates, but she sometimes phoned to break or postpone them.

Carter argued, "But if you started earlier in the morning you could finish—"

"I know. I know it's impractical, but it's the way I seem to have to work. I'm sorry. It's not something I can change."

Along with feeling some annoyance, Carter was moved and a little alarmed by her intensity, her high purpose.

Sometimes, in bed, Chase cried out quick, impassioned words of love to him—which Carter did not answer in kind, nor did he take what she said at those moments too seriously. In fact, as he was later forced to recognize, he gave rather little thought to Chase's deeper feelings. "You didn't want to deal with what I felt," she accused him, and he had to admit that that was entirely correct.

"Adam and I aren't getting along at all," said Meredith to Carter, over the phone. "I don't know—he's a lot more neurotic than I thought he was."

"Oh, that's too bad," was Carter's response. Not saying, *Now* you find this out, after wrecking our marriage and costing God knows what in lawyers' bills.

"He's very dependent," Meredith said. "I don't really like that. I guess I was spoiled by you."

"I don't know why she's telling me this stuff," Carter said to

Chase when she called; the old instinct of compulsive honesty had forced him to repeat the conversation with Meredith.

"I think she wants you back," Chase told him. "You wait and see."

"You think so? Really?"

"Jesus, Carter, you sound sort of pleased. If she did, would you even consider it?"

"Well, I don't know." As always, the literal truth; he did not know.

"God, Carter, she slept with everyone. Everyone in town knows that. Why do you think I insisted on safe sex?"

She was furiously excited, almost hysterical, Carter thought. She was out of control. A little frightening—but he only said, "Oh, come on, now."

"How tacky can you get!" Chase cried out. And then she said, "Look, don't call me, I'll call you, okay?" And hung up.

True to her word, she did call him—once, very late at night. "I've had some wine," she said. "I shouldn't be calling, I mean, otherwise I wouldn't. But I just wanted you to know a couple of things. One, I was really in love with you. God, if I needed further proof that I'm seriously deranged. I always fall in love with the most unavailable man anywhere around. Emotionally. Mean eyes, good shoulders. *Shit,* why did I call? Good night!" And she hung up, loud and clear. A ridiculous and quite unnecessary conversation, in Carter's view.

Now, in the afternoon sunshine, Carter looks about at all the roses and the scented white wisteria—at their lovely house and at unlovely, untrustworthy, but deeply familiar Meredith. He finds that, despite himself, he is thinking of Chase. Of her passion (those cries of love) and her scornful rage and of her final avowals (but she was drunk). Is it now too late? Suppose he went to her and said that he was through with Meredith, would she take him back? Would she ask him to come and live with her? (So far, she has never suggested such a thing.) Could they marry?

No is the answer that Carter gives to all these questions. No, Chase would probably not take him back, and no, there is no way he could afford to marry her. Even if he were sure that he wanted to. Chase is crazy—she must be crazy. Look at those paintings. There in the warm sunlight he suddenly shivers, as though haunted.

"Yes," he says to Meredith, although she hasn't spoken for a while. "Yes, okay. All right."

The Haunted Beach

The room, in this old, West Coast Mexican resort hotel, is unspeakably shabby—a window broken, the bedside table precariously leaning sideways—and not entirely clean. Led there by the aging, barefoot busboy, Penelope Jaspers, an art dealer, and Ben Bowman, a superior court judge, both from San Francisco, exchange a heavy look. In the bathroom, which is not quite as bad as she feared, Penelope, who had requested this particular room (she has been here before, though not for several years), tries a faucet: no water. And then back in the bedroom she finds no electricity. She can see from Ben's face, and his stance, that he is prepared to tough it out if she is, but Penelope has more at stake in this trip, for her a possibly dangerous return to old haunts (although she has changed a lot since then, she feels), and so she rather quickly decides that discomfort will be less than no help. She tells the busboy, Alfonso, who does not seem to remember her (or is he being tactful?), "Things don't seem to work in this room, Alfonso. Could we see another?"

Alfonso does not recognize Penelope; they look so much alike, these North American women. Pale and too thin, they dress either in pants or in immodest bathing costumes. This particular light-haired woman has a smile more pleasant than the rest, and her voice is soft—he thinks that he may have seen her before, although with a taller husband, who had no beard. North Americans quite frequently exchange their husbands and wives with each other, he has been told. Nevertheless, as pleasantly as he can, he tells the woman, whose Spanish is fairly good, for a gringa, that he will return to the desk for another key; he will show them another room.

Penelope and Ben smile at each other, quickly, tentatively, and she tells him, with a gesture, "This room, with the Farquhars in it, you can't imagine the difference. They always came for a month, you know, and put their things around." Not telling him, And Charles and I were in the room next door. Ben "knows" about Charles, a painter; knows that she came here with him often, and that she felt "terrible" when she and Charles broke up (terrible for a couple of years, in fact; but now she is really okay, she has told him that too). "The room even seemed bigger," she adds.

"Empty rooms look smaller." Ben is given to such stray bits of information.

"Lucky there's another room. We hope."

"Probably. This is off-season," he reminds her.

There is another room, seemingly at the top of the flight of steps they have just come down—and which now, following Alfonso and their luggage, they climb again, in the almost stifling, unaccustomed April sunshine, among the still bravely flowering bougainvillea vines.

Happily, the new room is extremely nice. A new structure has been built over the old, existing structures, over the tiers of rooms—over all of them, in fact, except the lower row, where the Farquhars, and next door Penelope and Charles, used to stay. This room is large and white, with an alcove for bathing, another space for reading, or lounging about, with two sofas and a table. A king-sized bed, and a broad porch out in front, with a table and chairs and hammocks—and a sweeping view of the bay, the brilliant sea and its enclosing hills of jungle trees. The sea and the view for which they have come, essentially, to this place.

And how fortunate, really, that they have this room instead of the old one that Penelope asked for, the Farquhars' room. How lucky that the lights didn't work, Penelope is thinking, and the water. If things had been just slightly better they would have stuck it out, and suffered. Ben wanting to please her, to be a good sport, and Penelope, for her pride, pretending that everything was fine. But this is perfect, she thinks. Here we are in San Bartolomeo, but not in the same room or near those rooms. It is simply a much better version of what I had before, she thinks. How fortunate, all around.

She asks Ben, "Do you want a swim?"

He smiles. "Well, why not?"

"I'm over him, really, finally, I think. If I just don't go back to Mexico I'll be all right, probably." Penelope said this to her closest friend from time to time, with decreasing frequency, in the years that succeeded her disastrous breakup with Charles, with whom she had lived for five or six years (depending on whether you counted the months of quarrelsome separations). She said it a couple of times after entering into a "relationship" with Ben, a more or less respectable, though bearded, judge. And then this spring, now about three years "after Charles," as Penelope still thinks of it, she finds herself on a trip with Ben, not only to Mexico but to San Bartolomeo itself, the beautiful scene of too much, the scene of too many scenes.

What happened was an airlines deal, promotional: Go anywhere in Mexico for $199. Penelope and Ben read this, and they both began to say, Why not? We need a vacation, swimming, warm weather. In San Francisco, a long mild dry winter had been succeeded by a cold wet dark spring. And then they began to eliminate places: well, obviously not Cancún, and Cozumel's so far away. Acapulco is horrible, and Vallarta's much too crowded. Until at last Penelope said, more or less to herself, Well, why not San Bartolomeo? It's so much in my mind, I have to go back there sometime, why not now? with Ben? with whom, on the whole, she got along rather well—though not lately; lately she had felt rough edges between them.

San Bartolomeo was where every January, for a week, she and Charles struck a truce, or nearly. No really bad fights. Where everything was beautiful: the flowers; the green, encroaching jungle; the white beach and the sea. And the Farquhars, an elderly, distinguished couple, he an astronomer, she an actress, both long retired, were in the cabin next door—unlikely but close, and valued, crucial friends for wild Charles and frightened Penelope. With Carlotta and Travis Farquhar, Charles tamed down, drank less, and shouted not at all; he was, in fact, his best, most imaginative, entertaining, generous, and sensitive self. And beautiful; Charles was always more handsome than anyone else around. Penelope, losing fear, was more friendly and talkative than usual (she felt this to be so, with the Farquhars).

For those weeks in San Bartolomeo there had been not only the balm of the Farquhars' company but also that of the place itself, its extreme tropical, flowery, seaside beauty. The long days of nothing to do but swim and walk and eat and take naps. And make love.

The Farquhars had died a couple of years ago—as a dedicated couple will, within weeks of each other. And why, Penelope wondered in the weeks succeeding confirmation of plans for their trip, hers and Ben's, why had she so specifically asked for the Farquhars' room? Did she imagine that she and Ben (they sometimes spoke of marriage) might become, eventually, such a couple? Or did she want to be right next to, but not inside, the room that she and Charles had shared so happily? (It *was* true, they had been almost always happy in San Bartolomeo.)

In any case, it does seem fortunate that they are to be in quite another room—although, on the way down to go swimming that first day, and every day after that, they walk right past that well-known row of rooms, the bottom row. Vines and bushes have been allowed to grow up almost to the porches, interfering, Penelope supposes, with the view from those rooms.

On the plane down from San Francisco, Penelope had chatted somewhat nervously to Ben, extolling the virtues and beauties of their destination—indeed, until he patted her arm and told her, "Pen, it's okay, I'm sure it will be all right."

One of the attractions described by Penelope was Rosa's restaurant, a beach shack, at the foot of the path up to their hotel. "Rosa is wonderful," Penelope told Ben. "Very small and dark, this burnished skin. And such a great cook, the best seafood. She's so energetic! With this slob of a husband who lolls around in very clean clothes that probably she ironed."

As they reach the foot of the path, that first day, there indeed is Rosa's: a concrete floor with a thatched lean-to roof, some tables and chairs. And, swinging out into the breeze, several rickety cages, each housing a drowsy, shabby-looking parrot.

And there is Rosa! recognizing Penelope. "Ah, amiga!" and rushing toward her, as Ben stands off at some distance, discreetly, on the sand.

They embrace, as Penelope thinks that she had not remembered Rosa as being so small. Rosa's head barely reaches Penelope's breast. And then, still embracing Penelope, Rosa bursts into tears. "My husband!" she cries out. "Now dead two years!"

"Oh, how terrible. My husband died too," Penelope lies—a double lie; she and Charles never married, and he did not die but ran off to Turkey, finally, with a pretty boy. She does not understand this lie that she herself has told.

"Ah, amiga." Rosa presses her closer, and then lets go.

"My friend Ben." Penelope gestures vaguely in his direction, as Ben, who knows no Spanish (and thus did not hear Penelope's curious untruth), smiles.

"Ah, good," says Rosa, vaguely.

"We'll see you later; we'll come down for dinner," Penelope promises.

"Good."

But Penelope senses that Rosa has already lost interest in her. Rosa only wanted to say that her husband had died, wanted the drama of that moment. Her husband, the slob in his clean freshly ironed clothes, whom Rosa loved.

Having promised, though, they do go down that night to Rosa's for dinner, Penelope in her long white flowered dress, bought years ago, down here, in a funny store recommended by Carlotta Farquhar. "You look really pretty," Ben tells her as they settle into rickety chairs, next to the view of the night-black, half-moonlit sea.

Rosa's has all been repainted, a bright yellowish green, but still the room seems much darker than before. At one end, the kitchen end, a large TV set emits a murky light and a lot of noise—a Mexican talk show, dancers in frilly costumes, tambourines, guitars, Rosa and a group of assorted, T-shirted adolescents—her children, now five years older than when Penelope last saw them, all huddled, transfixed. Rosa, who used to be always rushing in and out of the kitchen.

The food is good, good fresh fish browned in garlic, but not as good as Penelope remembered it.

Ben asks, "Have you ever been to Hawaii?"

"No, why?" Not asking, Do you wish we were there instead? already?

"I just wondered. I used to go there a lot."

"You liked it?"

"Oh yes. With, uh, Betty."

Betty is Ben's former wife, who behaved very badly; she drank, had affairs, all that. Ben almost never speaks of her, conveniently for Penelope, who does not wish to speak of Charles. She asks him, "Do you think of going back there?"

He hesitates—what Penelope thinks of as a judicial pause. "No, I guess not," he tells her.

The group clustered at the TV set seems indescribably sad, to Penelope. She considers the life of Rosa, a life of such hard work, so many children, but successful, in a way: her own good restaurant, there on the beach. Very popular with tourists; or she once was. But now seemingly all is in ruins; nothing is getting through to her but absence and pain, mourning, and noisy TV talk shows. Rosa is so terribly reduced that possibly she has indeed shrunk in stature, Penelope believes. In no sense is she now the woman she once was. All over Mexico, Penelope imagines, there must be women like Rosa, defeated women, bowing to sadness. The emotions that she herself felt after Charles were sufficiently like this to make her now shudder, and some shame for Rosa, for herself, for all of them makes her wish that Ben had not met Rosa in this state.

Ben and Charles are so totally unlike, as men, that Penelope almost never consciously compares them. Ben is dark, quite presentable but not handsome. He is thrifty, extremely thrifty. Intelligent rather than brilliant, tending to be quiet, almost taciturn. Judicial. His most annoying expression, to Penelope, is, "Well, I'd have to see the evidence on that."

His love for Penelope, a love to which he admits, though reluctantly, seems out of character, odd. At times Penelope can hardly believe in its truth, but then Ben is an exceptionally truthful man. She senses that he would prefer a more conventional woman, perhaps another lawyer?—but in that case what was he doing with crazy Betty?

He must wonder, it occurs to Penelope, if she is in fact thinking of Charles, and if so what in particular she remembers.

Actually, what Penelope most remembered about San Bartolomeo, in those years of not going there, was the flowers— the spills and fountains of bougainvillea, the lush profusion of bloom, in every color: pink red purple yellow orange. And the bright red trumpet vines, and other nameless flowers, everywhere.

This year, however, she notices on their way to breakfast that everything looks drier; the vines are brittle, the palm fronds yellowing. There are some flowers still, some hard fuchsia bougainvillea, but far fewer.

Can there have been a drought in Mexico that she had not read about, along with all that country's other, increasing problems? Corruption and garbage, pollution, overpopulation, and disease. Extreme, unending poverty.

In the dining room things are more or less the same. A buffet table with lovely fresh fruit, and boxes of American cold cereal. An urn of awful coffee, not quite hot. Pretty young maids, who take orders for Mexican eggs, French toast, whatever. Penelope scours the room for some maid that she knew before, but finds none, not beautiful Aurelia, or small smart friendly Guadalupe.

The other guests, on the whole, are younger than the people

who used to come here. Younger and less affluent looking. Many couples with small children. They are all probably taking advantage of the new cheap fares—as we are, Penelope thinks, at that moment badly missing the Farquhars, their elderly grace, their immaculate dignity. "You would have liked the Farquhars," she says to Ben—as she has several times before.

Down on the beach, the scene is much the same as always, couples or groups lounging in various states of undress around their palapas, with their bright new books or magazines, their transistors, bottles of beer, and suntan lotion. Too many people. Most of the palapas are taken; the only one available to Penelope is at the foot of the steps, near Rosa's.

"There's not a lot of surf," Ben comments as they settle into uncomfortable slatted chairs.

"Sometimes there is." Does he mean that he would rather be in Hawaii, where the surf is higher?

"Those boats look dangerous," he tells her.

Penelope has to agree. Back and forth, perilously close to the swimmers, small motorboats race by, some hauling along waterskiers, others attached to a person who is dangling from a parachute, up in the sky. The boats are driven by young boys, sixteen or seventeen, from the look of them, who often turn back to laugh with their admiring girlfriends, on the seats behind them. In fact Penelope has always been extremely afraid of these boats—though Charles reassured her that they would not hit anyone (laughing: "They never have, have you noticed?"). But this year there seem to be more of them, and they seem to come in much closer than before.

A young Mexican woman with a bunch of plastic bottles, strung together, comes up to their palapa and asks if they want to buy some suntan lotion.

No, thank you.

A very small girl with enormous eyes comes by selling Chiclets.

No, thanks.

"It's odd about vendors this year," Penelope tells Ben. "There used to be lots of them, and they had some good stuff. Carlotta got some incredible necklaces. There was one in particular, a tall pretty young woman in a white uniform, sort of like a nurse. She had a briefcase full of lovely silver things. Pretty opal rings; it's where I got mine." And she spreads her fingers, showing him, again, the two opal rings, one pink and one green, each with seeming depths of fire, each surrounded by a sort of silver filigree. "About ten bucks apiece," Penelope laughs. "Augustina, her name was. I wanted to get more rings on this trip, but I don't see her."

"Why more?"

"Oh, they don't last. They dull and come apart. But I suppose I don't really need them." Though thrifty, Ben no doubt disapproves of such cheap rings, or so Penelope imagines—the wives of successful lawyers, and certainly of judges, do not wear ten-dollar rings. And in a discouraged way Penelope wonders why they have come to Mexico together, she and Ben. Most recently in San Francisco they had not been getting on especially well; there was a string of minor arguments, the more annoying because of their utter triviality—where to eat, whom to see, what to do—arguments that had left them somewhat raw, on edge. It comes to Penelope that she must have expected some special Mexican balm; she must have thought that somehow Mexico would make everything come right, would impart its own magic. And she thinks, Alas, poor Mexico, you can hardly heal yourself, much less me.

"Well, how about a swim?" Ben stands up, so trim and neatly made, in his neat khaki trunks, that Penelope sighs and thinks, He's so nice, and generally good; do I only truly like madmen, like Charles? Even as she smiles and says, "Sure, let's go."

As always, the water is mysteriously warm and cool at once, both nurturing and refreshing—and green, glittering there for miles out into the sunlight. But perhaps not quite as clear as before? Penelope thinks that, but she is not entirely sure.

Despite a passing motorboat, this one lolling at low speed, its owner smiling an invitation, drumming up trade—Ben strikes out into deep water, swimming hard. For an instant Penelope thinks, Oh Lord, he'll be killed, that's what this ill-advised (probably) trip is all about. But then more sensibly she thinks, No, Ben will be okay. He is not slated to be run over by a Mexican motorboat (or is he?). She herself, more and more fearful as another boat zips by, this one trailing a large yellow inflated balloon, astride which six young women shriek and giggle— Penelope moves closer to a large, wave-jumping group of Americans for protection.

She persuades Ben to go back to Rosa's for lunch, but the day scene there is even more depressing than what goes on at night: the same blaring TV, same group clustered in front of it—in broad daylight, the sun streaming outside on the beach, the lovely sea not twenty yards away. Rosa hardly looks up as they come in. And the food is indifferent.

Walking up the path to their room, Penelope observes, again, the row of empty rooms. And she remembers an elderly couple, the Connors, friends of the Farquhars, who always took the room on this end, that nearest to the path, and sat there, calling out to their friends who passed. The lonely old Connors, now very likely dead. But how easy to imagine them sitting there still, he with his binoculars, she with her solitaire cards. And, in the room after next, Penelope and Charles, and in the next room the Farquhars. It seems impossible, quite out of the question, for all those people to have vanished. To have left no trace in this air.

Instead of saying any of that to Ben (of course she would not), Penelope says, "I do wonder how come Augustina's not around anymore. Her things were great, and she was so nice."

During their siesta Penelope has a most curious dream—in which she and Charles and Steven, Charles's beautiful boy, are all good friends, or perhaps she and Charles are the happy parents of Steven. The dream is vague, but there they are, the three of them—cornily enough, in a meadow of flowers. And, as Penelope awakes, the even cornier phrase, "Forgiveness flowers," appears somewhere at the edges of her mind.

Nevertheless, it seems a cheering, on the whole restorative dream, and she awakens refreshed, and cheered.

That night she and Ben walk into the town for dinner, a thing that she and Charles almost never did, and they find the town very much as it was: dingy, rutted, poorly lit streets leading toward the center, along which wary old men loiter, sometimes stopping to rest on the stoop of a darkened house, to smoke a cigarette, to stare at the night. Then stores, small and shabby at first, little groceries, ill-equipped drugstores, with timid souvenirs, faded postcards, cheap cosmetics. And then more light, larger and gaudier stores. More people. The same old mix of tourists, always instantly identifiable as non-Mexican. And Mexicans, mostly poor, some very poor, beggars, pitiful dark thin women, holding babies.

At their chosen, recommended restaurant, no table will be available for half an hour. And so Ben and Penelope go into the small, white, rather austere church that they have just passed.

A mass of some sort is going on; a white-robed priest is at the altar; everywhere there are white flowers. Penelope and Ben take back-row seats, and she watches as three little girls clamber all over their mother, who prays, paying them no heed. The girls and their mother wear churchgoing finery, black skirts and embroidered white shirts, and all the family's black hair is braided, beautifully. Whereas, the more Anglo-looking (less Indian) families in the church are dressed more or less as tourists are, in cotton skirts or pants, camp shirts, sandals.

Their dinner, in an attractive open court, is mildly pleasant. A subdued guitarist plays softly in one corner; there is a scent of flowers everywhere.

"Do you really think we should marry?" Ben asks, at some point.

At which Penelope more or less bridles. "Well no, I'm not at all sure; did I say that I did—?"

He pauses, just slightly confused. "I didn't mean you had, but—well, I don't know."

She laughs, "You mean, not in Mexico."

He looks less nervous. "Oh, right." He laughs.

The next morning, very early, Ben says that he wants to swim. "Before those damn boats are around," he quite reasonably says. "You too?"

"I don't think so." What she wants is just to lie there for a while, savoring the Mexican dawn, just now visible between the drawn window draperies. "I'll come down in a little while."

"Leave the key in the blue sack, okay?"

Penelope lies there, deliciously, for ten or fifteen minutes. Ben will want to swim for close to an hour, she knows. She lies there, thinking of nothing—and then she puts on her bathing suit, a red bikini, puts the room key in the small blue airline bag, and starts down the path—down past the empty row of rooms where they all used to stay (it now seems very long ago), past Rosa's restaurant, and out onto the beach, where she leaves the bag with the key on a table beneath one of the palapas. And she steps out into the water, the marvel of cool, of freshness. She thinks she sees Ben's dark head, far out to sea, but what she sees could as easily be a buoy.

She swims for a while, fairly sure that dark head is indeed Ben's. She waves, and whoever it is waves back. Looking to shore, for the first time she notices a sign, TOURIST MARKET, and she wonders what that is. She heads back in, stands up, and starts walking out of the water, up onto the beach.

She is trying to remember which palapa table she put the bag on, and does not remember. She does not see the bright blue bag on any table.

And slowly it registers on Penelope's frightened consciousness that the bag is not there. Gone. No key to the room. At the same moment, the moment of realizing her loss, she sees an old man, a sort of beach bum, wrapped in something orange, rags, hobbling down the beach. And Penelope, wildly out of character, for her, now thinks, I have to run after him, I have to chase that old man, who must have my key. Whether I get it back or not, I have to run after him.

And she does. She starts off down the beach, running as best she can, but clumsily, in the deep dry sand.

She is unused to running, but the man ahead of her is very old. She is gaining on him when suddenly he veers off the beach, to the left, and into the Tourist Market. Where Penelope follows, not far behind.

Getting closer, she begins to shout, "Stop! Stop!"

The market is a row of booths, now mostly empty, so early in the morning, but here and there a solitary figure pauses, putting aside a broom or a dusting cloth, a crate—to observe this chase. Penelope imagines herself, as she must look: A tall blond skinny

American woman in a red bikini, chasing after a poor old man, a derelict, hysterically shouting. Why should anyone help her?

But there, ahead of her, at the end of the row of rickety booths, to her surprise she sees the old man wheel and turn. He is standing there on one leg, a tattered old bird, maybe too tired to keep on running.

His dark, grizzled face is all twisted, one eye is gone, the skin closed over, and most of his teeth are gone. His mouth contorts, and the bright remaining black eye stares out at Penelope. A dying Aztec, she thinks. She thinks, *Mexico,* I should not have come back here.

Over one of the old man's shoulders a large old brown leather sack is slung, zippered up. In which there must be her blue bag. Her room key.

But what she (ridiculously) says is, "Did you happen to see my bag? on the table?"

"No—" His voice is tentative, querulous, but his eye is challenging, accusing, even. Perhaps it was not he who took her bag but someone else, earlier, while she was swimming.

Penelope finds no way to say, Open your sack up; let me see what you have inside. How could she?

She says again, "My blue bag, are you sure you didn't see it?"

"Yes." He turns from her.

Defeated, Penelope begins to walk back through the market booths, past a sort of workers' restaurant, just opening up, past more booths, with jewelry, scarves, leather—to the beach.

Where bearded Ben is getting out of the water. Shaking himself, like a dog.

He frowns a little at what Penelope tells him, but then he says, "Well, it's not too bad. We'll go up to the room, and you wait there while I go to the desk for another key. They should have given us two. As I said."

However, after the fifteen or twenty minutes that Penelope

has been standing there in the hallway, outside their room, in the gathering heat of the day, Ben comes back to inform her that it is not so simple, after all. They don't *have* another key. Honestly, Mexico. Someone has gone to find the housekeeper. God knows how long that will take. It's Sunday, remember?

Since there is no existing key to their room—many keys have been lost, they are told, or simply not turned in—the only solution to a keyless room is for Penelope and Ben to move into another room. Which, once the housekeeper has been found (an hour or so) and their old room wrenched open, they finally do: with the help of several maids they repack and move all their clothes.

The new room is lower down, and smaller, with less of a view. Not as nice.

However, they are only here for two more days. Ben and Penelope, over their much-delayed breakfast, remind each other of this fact.

That old man with his rags, his toothless twisted mouth, and his one defiant eye is in Penelope's mind all that day, however. How angry he must have been, she thinks, if he opened the blue bag, expecting money, to find nothing but an old key.

And was it, after all, that old man who took the bag, or someone else, some other stroller on the beach who had vanished in another direction before Penelope got out of the water?

That night in the bar a young woman, another American whom they have seen around, with her fat young husband and two very fat small children, comes up to them to say, "Are you the guys who lost a blue flight bag, with your room key? My husband found it, in back of that Tourist Market, and he couldn't find anyone to claim it, so he turned it in at the restaurant there. Just go and tell them it's yours."

The next morning Penelope, dressed, sets out for the Tourist Market. She approaches it from a back road she knows that passes Rosa's and leads to the corner where she and the ragged old man confronted each other. Where now for a moment she pauses, imagining him, and she looks around, as though he might have come back and been lurking around. But of course he has not; there is only the road, and back of the road the yellowing jungle brush, in the beating Mexican sun. Penelope continues to the restaurant.

A pleasant-faced, plump young woman tells her, "Oh yes, your bag. Right here."

Penelope thanks her very much, gives her some pesos, and walks on with her bag, in which she can feel the room key, still there. And she thinks again of the old man, how angry he must have been to find only a key. Crazily, for a moment this seems to Penelope unfair; she even thinks of trying to find that old man, to give him some money—and she smiles to think of what Ben would make of that gesture, combining as it would two of her (to him) worst qualities: thriftlessness and "irrationality."

She continues through the booths, until she is stopped by a display of rings. She bends over, as always hoping for opals—and sees that there are several: opal rings of just the sort that she likes, the lovely stones with their fiery interiors.

A pretty Mexican woman in a yellow sweater, dark skirt, asks if she can help. These rings are about twenty-five dollars for two, but still so cheap! and so pretty. Penelope feels a great surge of happiness at having found them. The rings seem a good omen, somehow, though she is not sure of what: of this trip? that she was right, after all, to come back to Mexico, and to this particular place?

Negotiations with the young woman concluded, rings chosen and pesos paid, Penelope then asks her, on some whim, "Did you ever know a very nice woman who used to sell jewelry along the beach, named Augustina?"

"But I am Augustina!" *Yo soy Augustina.* The woman laughs, and the two of them embrace.

"Ah, amiga," says Augustina.

"I didn't recognize you; you always wore that white uniform," Penelope tells her. "I bought these rings from you!" and she shows Augustina her hand.

"Amiga, this time you come back very soon," Augustina says.

"Oh, I will. Very soon. Augustina, thank you." And with her rings, and the bag with its key, Penelope walks back to the hotel.

Their new room, she realizes as she goes out onto the balcony for a dry bathing suit, directly overlooks the old tier of rooms, where once she stayed with Charles, next door to the Farquhars.

On their last night in San Bartolomeo, Ben and Penelope have dinner in the hotel dining room, where, as always, the food is very bad—and the view magnificent; glittering black water, down through palm fronds. Stars, and a partial moon.

"Well, it's not the worst place I've ever been," is how Ben sums up their trip. Judiciously.

"It was really okay," Penelope tells her closest friend, a couple of days later, on the phone. "I'm glad we went. As a matter of fact, I hardly thought about Charles. He wasn't there." Then she laughs. "Actually I didn't think much about Ben either. I don't think he liked it very much there. But I thought a lot about

Mexico." And then she adds, "But not thinking about Charles is the same as thinking about him all the time. If you see what I mean."

The friend does see.

"Anyway, the trip made me feel a lot better," Penelope continues. "About everything. More free." She adds, with a laugh, "I can't think why."

Great Sex

"And then of course there was, uh, great sex," says Sheila Williams, a young pediatrician, to her friend Alison Green. She is trying to explain the long presence in her life of a man who in many ways made her unhappy. Dick, a very smart, politically visible young lawyer, with whom she has just broken up. Dick is white, Sheila black. Small and neat and trim, from Roxbury, Massachusetts, Sheila is from a religious family, and tends to be somewhat prim; this conversation is unusual for her.

Alison is also young, although her long dark-blond hair, knotted up, is streaked with white. She edits a small art magazine, which does not take up a lot of her time. She is also an unmarried mother (Jennifer is four), which does take time. She has reacted to her friend's last remark, about great sex, in several ways: relief that Sheila is no longer seeing Dick, who sounds mean, and some surprise at the last phrase, "great sex"—that not being taken for granted by herself, or by anyone she knows. She further observes that "great sex" has become in some instances one word. "We had greatsex," some people say.

The two women are seated in a pretty, still-cheap French restaurant out on Geary Street, in San Francisco. Drinking white wine, as they wait for their dinner. They are long-term friends, with a shared Berkeley past, but busyness now prevents their seeing much of each other, and so their visits always have a catching-up quality; they discuss work, love affairs, Alison's daughter, and sometimes Sheila's two dogs—in a usually jumbled order; the categories overlap. Sheila, who is basically shy, reluctant as to personal revelation, has a lot to say about her work, which is at the San Francisco General Hospital and also involves the parents of her patients, most of whom are poor: black, Asian, or Hispanic. Some battered mothers. They do not ordinarily talk, Alison and Sheila, even generally about sex. It was unusual for Sheila to say what she had. But breaking up with Dick has made her more vulnerable, more open, perhaps.

Earlier they had been comparing their just-passed day; a bad one all around, they had agreed, bad for them both. Alison that morning had taken Jennifer to the airport, for a weekend in Santa Barbara with Alison's mother, the grandmother whom Jennifer adores. A friend of Alison's had been going there too and offered to escort Jennifer, who was thrilled at the whole prospect. But the planes were all delayed because of fog— planes to anywhere, Paris or Jakarta, Singapore or just Santa Barbara. Sheila had had terrible, terminal trouble with her car.

Nothing earthshaking for either of them, solvable problems, just annoying. Alison called and canceled her appointments, told her assistant to reschedule, and she finally put a very excited Jennifer on the plane. And Sheila called Triple-A for rescue, and in the meantime got a cab to her office.

But now, with the wine, Sheila's phrase about great sex begins to reverberate in Alison's brain. She has not been "seeing" anyone for at least a couple of years, and perhaps for that reason her mind returns to three instances of sex that was the greatest.

"Holy screwing," was how her first lover used to put it; he was a grad student at Berkeley, in mathematics; they smoked a great deal of pot together and made love effortlessly, wonderfully. Later, somehow, their connection fell apart, and he went East to a teaching job.

After that, graduated, Alison worked at part-time gallery jobs in San Francisco, and tried for journalism assignments. In that uncertain period of her life she fell in love with an older (twenty years older than she was) sculptor, semifamous, and with him too the sex was—great. An earthquake, with deeper aftershocks.

Out of bed they also got on well; much talk, many small jokes, and some glorious High Sierra hikes. They moved in together and planned to marry, "sometime, when we get around to it." But then he was killed, at the corner of Market and Franklin Streets, "senselessly," by a hit-and-run red-light runner, who was never caught but whom Alison, even now when she is "better," dreams of killing.

After that, for Alison there was hard work and some slow success—publication of articles in increasingly prestigious art magazines. And scattered, occasional love affairs. Sometimes great sex, sometimes not so great. And then, all inner wisdom notwithstanding, she fell in love with a man who was married— "happily," or at least comfortably enough, conveniently, so that he told her from the start that he could not, or would not, dislodge himself. Besides, there were three children. But with him, once more, there was holy, earthquake sex. She liked him very much, and he her. He worked in Washington, D.C., in an environmental agency, and often came to San Francisco—sometimes alone, sometimes not. Seeing each other was often difficult, but for a time they managed. Alison lived on Potrero Hill, conveniently near the freeway. And even an hour together was worth anything, they felt.

When Alison became pregnant, Jack was sympathetic: bad luck, he saw it as, and of course she would have an abortion.

Of course he would pay, and he would do everything possible, supportively.

But Alison could not. She had had one abortion, the result of carelessness during a somewhat feckless affair. She had voted and marched for women's right to choice. But this time she could not, not possibly. Jack quite reasonably argued that he too should have a choice, since the baby was also his—and Alison saw that this was true. Still, she had to go ahead with this pregnancy. And she did, and lovely Jennifer was born; sometimes Alison even thought that she had somehow known that this baby would be *Jennifer,* so beautiful, so loved.

Sheila, her friend, just then starting in pediatrics, became their doctor.

Now Sheila, really out of character, is still talking about great sex. And Dick, the man she no longer sees, who was an ungiving, emotionally stunted person, as Sheila had always known. "Sometimes I thought he got some sort of charge out of having a black girlfriend," Sheila said. "A liberal credential. *So* correct. But there were other sides to him. Moments of kindness, generosity, and these flashes of amazing insight. Enough of all that to make me stick around. What I'm saying is, he's not all bad." Sheila laughs, but her dark-brown eyes are wide and serious.

"We're supposed to think that no one is, aren't we?" Alison laughs too.

The waiter brings their food; they seem to have ordered a lot.

Somewhat later Sheila more or less continues. "I think it's these moments of nice, of goodness, that all men have, or almost all, and that's what keeps us around. We all think that that's the real person. That what we're seeing is a window into who he really is." She adds, "I mean it's one of the things. With really battered women of course there's also fear, no self-esteem, and often no money."

"Oh, you're right," Alison tells her. She is struck by what sounds wise and accurate, although she herself has not experienced much meanness from men.

"Battered women," Sheila now says. "People think, or some people think, they hang around for sex, but it's not that, mostly. I was always hoping that Dick would turn into the person I sometimes saw."

Alison finds herself very moved by the fact of Sheila saying all this; it is so unlike her to talk of intimate matters in this way. She is in fact more moved by Sheila herself than by what Sheila is saying, although she sees its truth. But possibly, also, Sheila is theorizing in part as a way out of pain?

Sheila now asks Alison, "You've got plans for your childless weekend?"

"I've got to work," Alison grins. "Probably I should have planned more." And indeed she should have, she now thinks. She is unused to weekends without Jennifer; it is not as though she had longed for such unfettered time.

The somewhat antiquated or at least other-era impression made by this restaurant, with its worn white linen tablecloths, white ruffled curtains, and fake white daisies in the decorative fake-brick windows—all that is increased by the music, which is thirties and forties; at the moment Charles Trenet is singing, "Vous—qui passez sans me voir—"

The room at this hour, about eight, is filling up. Alison, absorbed in their conversation, and then her food, has not paid much attention to the other guests.

But she looks up just in time to see a new couple come in, a short plump woman in black, a tall thin man with familiar shoulders. They come in slowly, as though in a horror film. Alison's own oft-imagined worst dream: Jack and his wife. At the instant in which she recognizes him he turns and sees her, and starts toward their table. As his wife, long bright blond hair swinging, goes on to a table across the room.

Smiling widely, as Alison also is, he arrives. He bends toward her—can he have meant to exchange a social kiss? Alison extends her hand, as she says, "How nice to see you. You remember Sheila?"

"Yes of course." He shakes hands with Sheila too, and says, "Nice place!"

They have been there together several times.

"Oh, very."

"Well, uh, everything okay?"

He must be asking, Is Jennifer okay? Alison nods, and then he is gone, and Alison feels the crocodile smile which has stretched her face recede.

She looks down at all the food on her plate, says, "I can't eat this," and she adds, "Oddly enough," with a very small laugh.

"Of course not." Understanding Sheila. "Take some deep breaths."

Alison does breathe deeply, managing too to glance across the room. At her. And she thinks, I'm prettier than she is. An out-of-character thought: Alison is not especially vain, nor for that matter is *pretty* the word for her, as she knows. She is often described as attractive, tall and thin, with an interesting, angular face. Good bones. But Jack's wife is too old for her very bright long blond hair, and too plump for her very short black dress.

Sheila, who has also managed a look, now whispers, "Could it be a wig?"

Alison laughs softly. "I suppose, but I doubt it." She adds, "Jesus, the end of a perfect day."

Four years ago—or five by now, it must be five—when Alison was pregnant, she and Jack quarreled a lot, and each said melodramatic, bad things to the other.

"You're ruining your life—"

"It's my life, you're completely insensitive—"

"You're crazy—hysterical—you have no sense—"

"I never want to see you again—just stay away—"

Since then, and since Jennifer's birth, there has been a polite, somewhat stilted, occasional exchange of notes—Alison's sent to Jack's office, of course, as in fact her notes always were. For a while he sent money, checks that in her high pride Alison never cashed. Besides, by then she was doing pretty well on her own. The magazine, though tiny, paid her a good salary; its backer needed the tax loss. And she sold more and more articles.

Jack had never asked to visit, although she assumed that he still came to San Francisco from time to time.

Now Alison asks Sheila, "What shall we do with all this food? Would your dogs eat it?"

"No, the bones are too small. We'll have the waiter wrap it and we can leave it in a package for some homeless person."

That night Alison's sleep is broken, very troubled. She is plagued with dreams that vanish at the slightest touch of her conscious mind. She believes that Jack has been the focus of these dreams, but she is not entirely sure; nothing is clear. And when in her waking mind she thinks of him, his image is confused, as possibly it always was. There is the sensual memory of him, his weight, his bones crushing into hers, the hot smooth skin of his back, in her clutching hands. And then there is the loud-voiced angry Jack, who insists that she have an abortion. She finds, though, still another man, Jack the kind and super-intelligent good friend, with whom for hours she discussed almost everything in life—the environment; their childhoods;

Bosnia, Zaire, and Haiti; Jack's relations with the Sierra Club and other local environmentalists; Alison's magazine; local painters. And sometimes, even, their own connection (both disliked the word *relationship*). They alternated between celebration (it was so good; they cared so much for each other) and sadness (it was necessarily limited; they could not, for instance, travel together, or, more to the point, live together).

Alison thinks too of what Sheila was saying, describing those windows of niceness that keep even battered women going (Did even O.J. have moments of niceness? she wonders). As she stuck around with a man who meant to and probably would stay married, for whatever responsible, guilty reasons of his own.

She wonders, What will I do when he calls tomorrow, as he most likely will? She thinks, At least Jennifer's out of town, I don't have to lie about that.

At breakfast, raw with sleeplessness, she decides to spend as much of the day as she can on a long city walk. When Jack calls, her answering machine will pick it up, and she can do as she likes. She does walk, in the bright cool windy day, fog lingering on all the horizons of the city. Perfect for walking. She hikes down to the Embarcadero, and along all that way to the Ferry Building, past the new incongruous row of palms, and the old decaying empty wharves.

When she gets home, having walked for a couple of hours, she finds no messages, not one on her machine. Digesting what feels like keen disappointment, not relief, she simply stands there in her kitchen for a moment, looking out to her view of the Bay Bridge, the bay, and Oakland hills. And the Embarcadero, where she just was.

The phone rings. She hesitates, answers on the third sound. Jack. After a polite exchange of greetings, he says, "In a way

I'm sorry about last night. I hope you weren't as shaken up as I was. But you know, I've wanted to see you. To be more in touch. And Jennifer—"

Some honest quality of pain in his voice is very moving to Alison; it was good of him to say that he was upset. She tells him, "I'm really sorry, Jennifer's down in Santa Barbara with my mother."

A long pause before he says, "Could I just see you for a little? I really want to."

She too pauses, and then says, "In an hour. I've just got back from a walk. I have to take a shower."

As he comes into her living room, and they shake hands—again, Alison observes what she had almost forgotten: that Jack is rather shy, and his glasses tend to slip down his longish nose. He is very tall, his posture bad, and he is still too thin.

He says, "You're really nice to let me—"

"Well, of course—"

"No, not of course—"

Both wearing their shy smiles, they sit down at opposite ends of her sofa (as they have before). Alison tells him, "Jennifer. I'm sorry she's not here; a friend was going to Santa Barbara for the weekend, Susan, I don't think you met her. And it seemed such a good chance for Jennifer, she likes Susan and she really loves her grandmother, and she thinks Santa Barbara is great, the beach and all—"

She is babbling to stave off the sudden and unaccountable tears that threaten her eyes, and her voice. Alison realizes this, but she is afraid to stop. She adds, "She's really nice—"

Looking at her with his slow shy smile, Jack says, "Of course she is."

"Well, tell me how your work's going! You're still happy in Washington, and mad at most of the Bureau?"

"Well, yes and no."

He talks for a while, and Alison does not hear a word he says, as she thinks, He's a very nice man; he really is. It wasn't "just sex," whatever that means. I think we can be friends, and he can come and see Jennifer sometimes. *Friends.* And I'm not going to cry, and we won't make love.

But Alison is wrong.

After she has made tea, Twinings English Breakfast, which they drink, and after a lot more civilized conversation, Jack gets up to go, and as, staring at her with his very dark, myopic, and beautiful hazel eyes, he starts to say good-bye, Alison distinctly hears the smallest catch in his voice, and she sees the effort at control that he makes.

Which is just enough, at last, to set off her tears—a minute before he truly meant to leave.

Jack puts his arms around her, intending comfort, friendliness, but it does not work out that way.

They begin to kiss, and minutes later they have moved to Alison's bedroom, where, on her bed, once more, they have great—the greatest sex.

Raccoons

Every evening, despairingly, Mary Alexander, a former actress, puts out tin bowls of food for Linda, her cat, who is lost: stolen, starving somewhere, locked in a strange garage—maybe dead. In any case, gone. And every morning, on the deck of her small house in Larkspur, California, Mary examines the bowls and sees that nothing is gone, and her heart seems to shrink within her, her blood to chill. Out there among all the pots of luxuriant roses, bright geraniums, and climbing, profusely flowering bougainvillea, Mary looks blindly at all that color, that bloom, and at her pretty house, in the rare fine August sunlight, and she mourns for Linda; she is inhabited, permeated with loss. She takes in the plates and washes them off; she makes and eats her own breakfast, and then goes out for a walk. She spends the day in an effort to pull herself together, as she looks and looks, and calls and calls for Linda. And then at night she puts out the food again, and she waits, and hopes. For lovely Linda, who is as beautiful and as shy as a little fox.

This is very neurotic, Mary lectures herself, rather in the voice of her very helpful former shrink, a gentle, kindly, and most courteous man from Louisiana, who spoke in those attractive accents, and whose sternest chiding was, "That's just plain neurotic." And he would smile, acknowledging that they both already knew she was neurotic; that very likely most people are, including himself.

For comfort, Mary sometimes thinks of a man she considers the least neurotic among her friends: Bill, a biologist. Internationally known, he goes to conferences all over; he does a lot of work in Africa on AIDS. Bill is absolutely devoted to Alison, his wife, herself a distinguished watercolorist. Bill is also intensely attached to Henry, their cat. Once, in fact (this is the memory from which Mary takes comfort), Henry was reported missing by their housesitter; Bill and Alison were on a rare vacation in Paris. Many transatlantic phone calls ensued; Bill was almost on the plane to come back from Paris, to walk every block of their San Francisco neighborhood—when, of course, Henry strolled into their house, insouciant and dirty. But Bill, this internationally famous scientist, had been poised to cut short a trip with his much-loved wife, to come home from Paris to look for Henry, his cat. All of which now makes Mary feel a little less crazy, less "neurotic," but no less sad.

Mary's own life, viewed by any friend or acquaintance, would be judged comparatively rich, and in many ways successful. Early days in New York included occasional Broadway parts, some off-Broadway, and mostly good reviews. Too little money, usually, and too many (but generally good) love affairs. Then the move to San Francisco, the Actors Workshop, and ACT, plus some TV ad work, boring but well paid. More love affairs, some of which became rewarding friendships. Even now, at what she herself considers an advanced age, there is a man with whom she sometimes sleeps (Mary much dislikes the phrase *to have sex,* but they do), a man of whom she is most extremely fond (which surely beats being in love, has been Mary's conclusion). They would see each other more, except that he has a very mean, vindictive lawyer wife; it is not all perfect, but then, what is? In any case, Mary's life does not fit the stereotype of the lonely old woman whose only companion is her cat.

Mary was never beautiful; as a very young woman she was too thin, almost gaunt, with a long thin nose, a wide and sensual mouth. But she was both intelligent and talented, capable of projecting passion, irony, and humor, qualities that she could be said to contain within herself. Her friends, including fellow actors, generally liked her, and several men loved her extremely.

Aging is easier, somewhat, for a not-beautiful actress, Mary has thought; critics are less apt to point out that you are not as young as formerly. But this must be true for all women, not only those in her own narcissistic profession? You do not suddenly observe that heads are not turning, if few or any ever did. These days Mary could have more TV ad work than she does, if she would accept more happy-grandmother shots. The problem is that her capacity for tolerating boredom has diminished, she finds. She can no longer endure certain endless hours before hot cameras—as she can no longer listen raptly at dull dinner parties. She cannot escape into steamy trash fiction as she once did, in dressing rooms, awaiting calls. (She has lately been rereading Colette, and has recently discovered Carl Hiaasen, who makes her laugh aloud.) The move from San Francisco up to Larkspur constituted a sort of retirement; she lives mostly on residuals, a little stock. She believes that she lives fairly well, with Linda.

Still, certain things have happened, inevitably, to her face and body that she does not like, and cannot much change. Mostly she objects to dry skin, and increasing fatigue.

Mary has—or she used to have, with Linda—certain small rituals. Rituals of love and intimacy, you might say. One was that whenever Mary went upstairs, Linda would race ahead of her, and then stop and lie across a step, in Mary's way, so that Mary had to stop. And to pet Linda, to scratch her beautiful yellow stomach as Linda stretched along the step. They always did this, and now, as Mary walks up the stairs alone and unimpeded, she misses Linda as acutely as she has ever missed a lover, and she thinks, in somewhat the same way as she used to think, He's gone!

So that now she thinks, I must be truly mad. All this about a pretty little cat? I carry on as though it were a major love affair?

Linda now has been gone for five days, and nights. Mary continues her nightly routine of putting food out on the deck and bringing in the untouched dishes in the morning. Washing them out.

Getting through the days.

And then one night, as she lies upstairs in bed, alone, she hears from down on her deck the rattle of tin plates—her plates, with Linda's food. *Linda!* In an instant she grabs up a robe, shoves her feet into slippers; she runs downstairs and flicks off the burglar alarm. She rushes to the french doors that lead to the deck. Where she sees, to her horror, three raccoons. Two large, one smaller, all with their round black staring unfrightened eyes and their horrible bent clawed feet. At times Mary has argued that raccoons are cute, nice little visitors at picnics. But tonight she sees that they are hideous intruders, feral and dangerous, fearsome.

She is afraid that if she opens the door they will run in, searching for more food (they have eaten all of Linda's), and so she only bangs on the glass, afraid too that it will break, and she will be defenseless. But the raccoons, having eaten, now leave, loping, ungainly on their short legs and ugly feet, back across the deck.

Very slowly Mary goes upstairs, and gets back into bed.

Raccoons attack cats; they sometimes hurt or kill them. Everyone says that.

Mary gets up, and in her bathroom she takes a tranquilizer, then gets into bed again.

She lies there, coping as best she can with the probable fact of Linda's death (later she does not understand how she did this). Linda must be dead, killed by horrendously ugly, murderous raccoons; if not those, some others, equally hideous. Mary only hopes that it was quick, as one hopes for air-crash victims. Poor crazy fearful Linda could well have died of fright before she was hurt, Mary thinks.

She tries to sleep, and at last she does, and she wakes in the morning very calm, and much, much more sad.

And although she has more or less accepted the fact of Linda's death, she continues in a minor way to look for her, and she still puts out the food.

"What you need is another cat," the few friends in whom she has confided begin to say, and in theory Mary agrees; she does need another cat.

One day (it is now September, Linda gone for a week) the sun comes out earlier than usual, burning through fog and leaving only a few white mists that hang above the tall dark trees, above the town of Larkspur. Mount Tamalpais is sharp and clear, less distant, more inviting. And Mary's mail comes earlier than usual, just before lunch. In it there is a check that she has been owed and has needed for some time, from her agent in L.A. These are all good signs, she thinks; Mary has certain unvoiceable, eccentric superstitions. Perhaps this should be the day when she goes to the animal shelter and finds a new beautiful cat.

She cannot resist the further superstitious thought that *maybe* getting a new cat will bring Linda magically home to her, rather in the way that couples with a fertility problem at last adopt, and then become pregnant.

In the animal shelter, which is encouragingly clean, well kept up, and staffed by very nice and cheerful young women, Mary looks through the rows of cages, all containing cats with one or another sort of appeal, any one of whom she would no doubt in time learn to love. But no cat there is as beautiful as Linda is (or was); there is no one whom she instantly, totally loves. In the last cage, though (of course the last), there is a thin, lithe, graceful gray cat named Fiona—to Mary an appealing name; years ago she had a friend, an English actress, Fiona Shaw (just as she once had a friend named Linda, years back). A small typed notice states that Fiona has just been spayed; she is fine, but not quite ready for adoption—a few days more. Mary watches Fiona for a little while; she is an exceptionally pretty little cat, shy and graceful. (And if Linda *should* come back, they might get along?)

On the way home Mary sees some new neighbors, a nice young couple, both architects, who have heard and been kind and sympathetic over Linda.

"I saw this very pretty cat in the shelter," Mary tells them. "A small gray one. She's named Fiona."

Almost in unison they say, "But Linda might come—"

"No," Mary tells them, very firmly. "The raccoons got her. They must have."

At which the young man frowns. "I've seen a couple around. Mean-looking little bastards."

And the woman, "I think they're sweet. And I could have sworn I heard a cat outside last night."

"Well, you'll have to come for tea very soon and meet Fiona," Mary tells them.

Every return to her house, which now does not contain Linda, is sad for Mary, and as she walks in, the raccoons now return to her mind, unbidden; she sees them vividly again, their hideous claws and their small mean shining eyes. Firmly she forces herself instead to imagine pretty Fiona as she walks through her house to the deck, and down the steps to her garden.

Where she is just in time to see a flash of brown fur, a plumey tail—Linda!—who tears across the grass and into Mary's basement, which contains a clutter of broken, discarded furniture, empty boxes, old luggage. Where Linda instantly hides herself.

The basement entrance is wide, with no door; there is no way to block it off, to prevent a bolting Linda—except for Mary herself to stand across it, or to sit down, as she does, and to stretch her legs across the opening.

But was that really Linda, that flash of fur? Mary begins to doubt her own vision. Could it, God forbid, have been a raccoon?

In her softest, most caressing voice she calls to Linda; she calls and calls, a stream of loving syllables that Linda must know (if cats know anything) and always her name. "Linda, Linda-loo, lovely Linda—" On and on, with no answer.

She would like to go upstairs and phone the nice neighbors for help; she could block the escape route while they went in and banged around, but she does not dare leave. She would also like a glass of water. But she has to go on. "Linda, loopy Lou, Linda-pie—" On forever.

At last, after maybe ten minutes, there is a sort of rattling among the boxes; an old broken bamboo table moves, so that Mary sees a glimpse, a quick tiny glimpse, of what is surely Linda.

After another five minutes, probably, of calling, and of small but increasingly certain sighting, Linda emerges into a small cleared space, a safe twenty feet from where Mary sits. Linda emerges, she stares, and retreats.

She repeats all that several times, each time flicking her tail, back, forth.

And then she emerges into another, smaller space, about ten feet from Mary. Looking at Mary, she rolls over—the first sure friendly signal, or even acknowledgment that she has ever seen

Mary before. She does this three or four times, each time some-how managing to roll through still poised for flight.

And so Mary does not reach out to grab her, restraining her-self until she is absolutely sure of reaching and grasping Linda. Which at last she successfully does, with a firm, strong, loving, and furious grip.

"You rotten little slut, where in God's name have you been, you little bitch?" She whispers these harsh new words, rising and clutching Linda, who is struggling hysterically to get away— away from this sudden stranger who has seized her unawares.

But this time Mary wins. She carries fighting Linda out of the basement, up the stairs, and across the deck and into her house.

Dumping her onto the rug she asks, "Oh Linda, how come you're so *crazy*?" and, again, "Where on earth have you *been*?" No answer.

And Linda, in character, runs off and hides. She does not even seem very hungry, nor does she have the look of a starving lost cat. She has obviously done well for herself, but Mary will never know where, or how. Or *why*. Mary pours herself a glass of white wine and collapses on the old chintz sofa, thinking, God*damn* Linda, anyway.

How much, or what, do cats remember? Can anyone com-prehend at all the memory of a cat? Over the next few days Mary wonders and ponders these questions, sometimes staring into the round yellow eyes of Linda as though there might be a clue. As though Linda knew.

She considers too the fact that both she and her friend Bill the biologist have chosen cats of their own gender for major loves. Could this mean that love of one's cat is really love of one's self? Was it she herself who she feared was lost and hungry, pos-sibly dead?

At other times she simply holds her hands around that small warm vibrant body, the delicate strong ribcage and the drum-tight rounded belly, and she thinks, and she says aloud, "You're home, darling Linda. You came *home*."

Mary has had the wit not to talk much to her friends about the loss of Linda, and so now she does not make much of her return. Only to her sometime lover, who is also in a way her closest friend, she confides, "I'm embarrassed, really, when I think how upset I was. And that night when I was sure the raccoons had got her, well—"

"Mary dear, you were great," he says. As he might have said, as people did say, of some performance of hers, which, come to think of it, in a public way it had been. No one really knew that for Mary the loss of Linda had been the end of the world, or nearly. None of her friends or her lover knew that she would have sacrificed any or all of them for her cat.

Or at least at moments she would have.

Soon after Linda's return there is a small dinner party for some visiting old friends from New York, and at which Mary very much enjoys the sort of theatre gossip that she is used to: "But Maria's always great. . . . I hear Edward's new play is even better. . . . Poor Colin is really sick. . . . No, Gilbert's still okay . . . they are not getting a divorce . . . the problem was that she loathed L.A. . . . I must say, you're looking wonderful. . . ." She comes home in a mood of slightly wistful but pleasant nostalgia. She goes upstairs and finds Linda, as usual, curled on the foot of her bed. She pats Linda, who looks up, blinks, purrs briefly, and goes back to sleep. Soon Mary too is sound asleep.

She wakes an hour or so later, and at first she thinks, I should never have had that last glass of wine, I didn't need it. I know I can't drink red. But then she hears a scratching, rustling sound on her deck, which may have been what woke her up.

She gets out of bed, slowly puts on slippers and robe, noting as she passes that Linda is not there. She goes downstairs, flicks on lights—and there on her deck, lined up, are four raccoons, one large, three smaller. They keep a certain distance, and perhaps for that reason are not quite as threatening as they were before. They look both formal and expectant; they could be either judges or penitents—impossible to tell. Or, they could be asking for Linda. Demanding Linda?

Mary turns off the lights and goes back upstairs, where she does not find Linda anywhere in her bedroom; she even looks under the bed. She spends an anxious half hour or so in this search for Linda, at this ungodly hour, at the same time telling herself that this is ridiculous. There is no way that Linda could have gotten out; all the doors are locked, her bedroom window is only opened a crack. She also thinks: I cannot go through this again, I really can't—as she calls out softly, "Linda, darling Linda, where are you?"

She at last finds Linda asleep on the studio couch in her study, a not unlikely place for her to be, though more usual in the daytime. As Mary approaches, Linda wakes and raises her head; she blinks and looks at Mary as though to say, This is the middle of the night; I was sleeping here quietly. What is your problem?

The next night, after feeding Linda, Mary is moved to put out a little food for raccoons, really for whatever creature wants it. She puts a little plate of dried kibble and one of water down in the garden, where she cannot hear if the plates are rattled.

And whether the impulse that moved her is one of simply nurturing or of a more complex propitiation, or some dark exorcism, Mary has no idea.

Old Love Affairs

Mildly upset by a phone call, Lucretia Baine, who is almost old but lively, comes back into her living room and stares for a moment into the large white driftwood-framed mirror there, as though to check that she is still herself. Reassured, she smiles briefly, but continues to look at the mirror. In the soft, kindly lamplight—this is an early evening, in October—she is beautiful, still, even to her own harshly critical (large, green) eyes. But she knows perfectly well how she looks in her cruelly accurate bathroom mirror, first thing in the morning. Now, though, she looks all right, just upset; on the other hand, she may look better than usual. A little more color?

The disturbing call did not involve bad news; it was simply that Lucretia momentarily confused two men: Simon, whom she is crazy about (hopelessly, irreversibly, it seems), with Burt, who in his way is crazy about her. He loves Lucretia permanently, he says. Burt called, and just for an instant she thought he was Simon. Although she would have thought that two men more unlike did not exist, including their voices: Burt's deep and friendly, Midwestern, and Simon's very New England, Cambridge, slightly raspy.

"Crazy about." Like many people, Lucretia tends to think in

the argot of her youth, in her case the forties. However, in this instance, the instance of Simon, the phrase seems accurate. At her age, to harbor such feelings is crazy indeed, and so, for that matter, are Burt's feelings for her, at his advanced age. Lucretia sighs. If only Simon were gay and in love with Burt the circle would be perfect, Shakespearean, she thinks. She sighs again, at what seems the silliness of it all. Simon is not gay, and the two men have never met. And she only confused their voices because she was expecting a call from Simon, sort of.

She did not do anything so crude as calling Burt "Simon"; she was only a little cool at the onset of the conversation, cool with disappointment. But then poor Burt was probably used to cool, from her.

This living room of Lucretia's, though comfortable and exceptionally pretty, too often called "charming," in a sense resembles an archaeological dig; there are layers, and remains. Traces of former husbands, three of them, two divorced, one dead. Tokens and presents from former lovers, quite a few of those, and from good friends, even more. And clear signs of a long and steadfast career: Lucretia is a reporter, a dedicated newspaperwoman. She has always worked in that way. The driftwood mirror is, in fact, a present from her longtime editor, now an elderly gentleman, who is gay—a much-loved friend; Lucretia is less sure how she feels about the mirror.

Thus the room, which has never exactly been "decorated," is full of trophies, of carefully, tastefully selected objects, and of whimsically, impulsively bought *things*. A jumble of books and pictures, lots of framed photographs; anyone can see that Lucretia, young, was quite ravishing, and that most of the men she knew were tall and good-looking. Pots and vases of flowers stand about, more carefully arranged than they look to be: a great clump of growing gold chrysanthemums, smelling of earth, and of fall—and a slender silver vase of yellow roses, unscented but beautiful, chosen by Lucretia, for herself. She sometimes wonders how she could feel lonely in such a room, and, for that matter, in such a house, but sometimes she does.

Souvenirs, then, of love and friendship, but also of work. Lucretia has done a lot of travel writing for many years, as the assistant travel editor of her paper; shelves of travel books, as well as atlases and stacks of maps, attest to those years, along with one wall's collection of masks, from Mexico and from Haiti, from India and Africa and Egypt. For idle pleasure Lucretia sometimes picks up a map of Italy, say, and goes over it carefully, naming out favorite towns to herself: Orvieto, Todi, Arezzo, Fiesole, as another person might read a familiar novel, happy to recognize Barsetshire again.

She was working throughout all those marriages and love affairs, which no doubt kept her sane (she herself is sure of this), but these days her work creates certain problems in "relationships" when the men involved are retired, as Burt is—Burt especially, demanding, intrusive (more "in love"), does not like to hear about Lucretia's deadlines, her work obligations. He has often suggested that she retire. What he means is, marry him. But Lucretia plans to postpone retirement for as long as she can, and in the meantime to take whatever assignments the paper offers. She has gone back lately to doing more interviews than travel writing, although last December she wrote a long piece about Christmas in Venice, lights in the Piazza San Marco, processions of gondolas. Extremely handsome gondoliers.

Lucretia's first marriage took place when she was eighteen. There should be a law against marriages under thirty, she has sometimes thought, and said. Surely under twenty, and probably twenty-five. Jim, the young husband, was in law school; her second, Tommy, a reporter. Years later, speaking of marriage, she also said, "I married the first two times for sex. How dumb can you get?" Sometimes adding, "Tommy was dear, well, really they both were, Tommy and Jim. But Tommy drank so much, and besides, I really needed to get out of Boston."

She divorced poor, dear Tommy in Reno, and continued to San Francisco, where, with some money from a grandmother who providentially died around that time, she bought a small house in an alley on Telegraph Hill—with such a view! And she got a job on the *Examiner*.

There then followed for Lucretia many happy years. Telegraph Hill and, indeed, the whole city were seemingly full of the relatively young and unmarried. There was great cheap Italian food and wine in North Beach restaurants, and great cheap Chinese along Grant Avenue, Chinatown, with wonderful jazz at the Blackhawk, the Jazz Workshop. And good bars all over the place. Not to mention the prettily romantic city itself, a perfect backdrop. Lucretia had quite a few very pleasant but not serious love affairs; to herself, she thought, Well, good, I'm beginning to take sex not quite so seriously; it's just very good, very affectionate fun.

Sometimes, though, she was assailed by much darker thoughts, one of which persistently was: I'm really too old for all this silliness; my friends are doing serious things like bringing up children. (In those days thirty-five was viewed as too old for almost anything, including love affairs and certainly children.) Also, the fact was that she still did take sex seriously. Her affairs were never so casual as she tried to make herself believe; she sometimes suffered extreme pangs of missing whoever was just gone. Pangs of longing to hear from someone who did not phone. (In those days women were not supposed to telephone men.)

In those blacker moods Lucretia tended to forget her own considerable professional success. She was extremely good at

her work; she had won citations and prizes, along with the occasional raise. And she liked it very much, especially the interviews, which she was more and more frequently assigned. She
liked the work and mostly she liked her fellow reporters. But as
she waited for her phone to ring, waited for *him* to call, she forgot all that.

Jason was first described by Lucretia to her friends as "this
terribly nice man who lives next door." A tall, skinny young (her
age) architect from Tennessee, Jason had a serious girlfriend,
Sally, who was not around much. Jason and Lucretia went to
movies at the Palace and to the New Pisa for long, half-drunken
dinners together; when she broke up with whomever, Jason was
always comforting. And she was nice to him, making homey
meals and listening a lot when he broke up with Sally, although
by then Lucretia was seeing someone else.

By the time they fell in love and decided to marry, Jason and
Lucretia had been friends for several years. So sometimes she
wondered, Why didn't I know all along how I felt about Jason?
Why did we waste all that time?

In both earlier marriages, to Jim and then to Tommy, sex had
been the greatest bond. Especially with Tommy, a true sexual
explorer, an inspired and tender lover—when sober. But then,
he was so often drunk. With Jason, after the early raptures of
mutual discovery, when in effect they both said, "You've been
here all along, and I didn't *know*?—after some months of that,
the sexual energy between them seemed to taper off to a twice-
a-week nice treat. Lucretia often felt that she was more enthusiastic than Jason was, that perhaps she was basically a sexier
person, which she found a little embarrassing, although she still
liked Jason better than anyone in the world. And for the three
years of their marriage they were mostly happy, both busy with
separate work, and enjoying vacation trips together.

Then, cruelly, Jason, who was still a relatively young man,
was diagnosed with colon cancer. Invasive. Inoperable. But he

took a long time dying, poor darling; near the end Lucretia moved him down to the living room, where he could see the friends he still wanted to see, and she could more easily bring him trays. He complained sometimes about sleeping down there alone, and so Lucretia would cuddle against him, there on the couch.

Unhappily, that is what she most clearly recalled of Jason, his dying. How pitifully thin he was, his eyes so huge and needful. His bony hands. She remembered less of his good jokes and general good sense. Their trips. Lovely Italian wine and, at times, good sex.

Mourning Jason, a truly loved and irreplaceable friend, Lucretia mourned, too, what she felt to be the end of love in her life. By that time she was in her early fifties; even to think of love affairs was ridiculous, despite what she read here and there. And so she did something very ridiculous, or worse: she fell violently in love with a man almost twenty years younger than she was, a beautiful Italian, Silvio. Not only twenty years younger but married, and a Catholic, of course.

Oddly enough, it was he who loved first. Or he who said it first, pressing her fingers as they held a wineglass, at lunch, in Fiesole. Looking up at him, she saw him laugh in a slightly embarrassed way as he said, "You mustn't laugh, although it is a little funny. But I find myself seriously in love with you."

She did not laugh, but she smiled as she said, "Oh Silvio, come on—" even as her heart began to race, her blood to surge forward.

She was aware that they looked a little alike, she and Silvio, a northern blond; some people must think them mother and son. Many people must think that.

Lucretia was staying at a small hotel on the Arno, not far from Harry's Bar; she had a penthouse room, with a lovely view of the river. From her balcony, in early evenings, she observed the long ovals formed by the bridges and their reflections in the water. She and Silvio had drinks there the first night he came to call, quite properly, to take her to Harry's for dinner. He was the friend of a friend; his wife and children were off at Viareggio. After they became lovers, they had drinks on that terrace every night.

"You have the most marvelous skin in the world," he told her. "Your back, and here. Like hot velvet." He laughed. "My poor English. I sound like the TV."

"Your English is fine."

"You are fine. However can I let you go?"

But he did. They let each other go at the end of Lucretia's two weeks: a week of exploratory friendship, another of perfect love. Or, vividly recalled by Lucretia in San Francisco, that is what it seemed, all perfect. Beautiful, sexy Silvio made love to her repeatedly, over and over, at night, and then again in the morning, before driving off to his own house across the river. Just love and sex; they never spoke of anything foolish and alien, like divorce. Only, once or twice Silvio asked her, "If I should come to San Francisco, you will remember?"

She laughed at him. "Always, my darling." She feared that that would indeed be true. And she thought, Suppose he calls when I'm really old, too old to see him again, although I still remember? (She forgot that at that time he, too, would be much older.)

In her pretty Telegraph Hill cottage, then, with the doleful sound of foghorns strained through her dreams, Lucretia often woke to a painful lack of Silvio, a missing of him that was especially sexual. And none of the obvious solutions to this crying need appealed to her at all. Only Silvio would do, and at times, at the worst and most painful predawn hours, she thought of flying back to Italy. To Florence, where she would say to Silvio what seemed at the moment to be true: I can't live without you.

Of course, she could and did live without him, and all the prescribed cures worked. She joined a health club and exercised fiercely; she walked whenever and for as long as she could. She intensified her efforts at work; she took on more assignments. And she thought, Well, that will have to be that. Enough of sex and love. I've surely had my share, and maybe more. Except that every now and then she would read some tantalizing, romantic account of a woman even older than she was falling in love, getting married. Or an article about the sexual needs and activities of the old. "Geriatric Sex." Lucretia's very blood would warm and flare, and she would think, Well, maybe. Even as a more sensible voice within would warn her, Oh, come *on*.

"He's not exactly your type, but he's nice," said a friend, by way of introducing Burt McElroy into her life. "He's dying to meet you."

"Good Lord, why?"

"Oh, don't be like that. You're sort of famous here, and he likes blonds. His wife was blond."

"Old blonds."

"His wife was older than you. They were married forever."

"I just don't feel like meeting anyone. I've given up all that stuff. Or maybe it's given me up."

"Well, just come for dinner. I won't lock you up in a closet together or anything." She added, "He was a trial lawyer. Now retired."

The lawyer, Burt McElroy, was a very large man, at least six three, and heavy. Thick white hair and small bright-blue eyes, a big white beard. Jolly, at first glance, but on second not jolly at all—in fact, somewhat severe. Censorious. And a little sad.

At dinner that first night, at the house of the friend, Burt talked considerably about his wife, and a music foundation that he was establishing in her honor; apparently she had been a noted cellist. As he spoke of this dead woman, this Laura, Burt often looked at Lucretia, and she understood that he was announcing his feelings: I will never be really untrue to Laura.

And so she laughed, and was flirtatious with him; she, in her way, was saying, "Look, don't worry, I'll never be serious about you either."

A few days later he called and asked her out to dinner. They went, and again he talked a lot about Laura and his children. At her door he said, "You know, you're really a knockout lady. As we said in my youth, 'I could really go for you.' "

"Oh, don't do that." She laughed up at him.

Later, thinking over the evening, Lucretia saw that she did not like him very much, despite his good qualities. He talked nonstop and rather self-importantly, a man accustomed to having the floor. To delivering opinions. And he did not listen well; in fact, he showed very little curiosity about her or anyone else. In short, he bored her; it was true, he was not her type at all. Except for being tall.

But she recognized, too, with some shame, a certain sexual pull in his direction. She looked forward to when he would kiss her. She put this down to sheer sexual starvation—it had been a long time since she had kissed anyone.

Their next dinner was less boring for Lucretia, because of the kissing that she now looked forward to. Just that, kissing, for the moment.

They went from a good-night kiss at the door to some very enthusiastic kissing on the sofa, and then, because such adolescent necking seemed ridiculous at their age, they went to bed.

Where, after several long, futile minutes of strenuous efforts on his part, and some effort on hers, Burt said, "I'm sorry. I had this prostate surgery, and I was afraid, but I had hoped—"

He was breathing hard, from exertion rather than from lust, Lucretia felt, as she thought, Poor guy, how embarrassing this must be. And depressing.

"Here," he said. "Let me—" He moved heavily, laboriously, down her body, positioning himself.

This is not something he usually does, Lucretia thought. Oral sex was not on the regular menu with Laura, the wife. Though, of course, Lucretia could have been wrong.

Feeling sorry for him, she pretended more pleasure than she actually felt; also, she wanted him to stop.

He moved up to lie beside her; he whispered into her ear, "It's wonderful to give you pleasure. You're wonderful."

Without spelling things out, without saying, "Look, I'm sorry, but I just don't like you very much. And sexually, I know it's not your fault and I'm sorry you have this problem, but it just doesn't work for me. I'm sorry I pretended," Lucretia hoped he would somehow understand. It did not occur to her until later that she could just have not seen him again, without apology.

Because he did not understand; he seemed now to want to see her all the time.

He took her to a banquet at which he was the guest of honor, long tables at the Fairmont Hotel, important political people. Men whose names, at least, she knew.

Lucretia, in her proper, "appropriate" black dress and her proper pearls, felt fraudulent; she wanted almost to announce: I'm not his lady friend, we are not, not, *not* getting married.

Burt's friends were roughly the same age as Lucretia was, like Burt himself, but they all seemed considerably older. She thought this could be delusional on her part, a delusion of youth, although she knew that she was generally a realist in that way. Vain, perhaps, she surely was that, caring too much about how she looked. But not kidding herself that she was a kid anymore.

She was not quite sure what this "older" quality consisted of; the best she could do was to describe it as a sort of settled heaviness, in both minds and bodies. They all looked pleasantly invulnerable, these people, Burt and his friends. No longer subject to much change. Or to passion. They did not much mind being overweight. Or that their expensive clothes were out of style.

Lucretia was not exactly smug about looking younger, and better; she knew it was largely accidental. She had been born pretty, and most of it had lasted. She ate almost what she wanted to, and nevertheless stayed fairly thin. She exercised, but not immoderately. She had not had anything "done" to herself in a surgical way, although she had thought about it.

"You're the sexiest women I ever met. I'm crazy for you," Burt breathed into her ear.

"But—"

"Maybe a little cruise somewhere? Alaska, maybe, or Baja."

"Cruises—"

"Look, forget you're a travel writer. Just come along. Enjoy."

At the time of the cruise conversation (she had been on a number of cruises and very much disliked them all) Lucretia was much involved in writing a series of articles on shelters for battered women. She tried to tell Burt just how involved she was, how she cared about this particular piece.

Which did not go over well with Burt. "You should throw your weight around more," he told her. "Such as it is," and he laughed at his own mild joke. He often teased her about being what he called "underweight." "You've been there long enough and won enough prizes," he scolded. "You should be calling the shots. Not taking these really tough assignments."

I'm trying my best to call the shots with you, she thought, but did not say. And I like writing this piece; I like these women.

It was Burt's mouth that gave his face its severity, she

decided. A small mouth, set and firm, made smaller-seeming by the surrounding beard. Had someone long ago said that small mouths were a bad sign, that they meant an ungiving, stingy nature? Actually, Burt was somewhat stingy, she had come to see; "careful" would be the kinder word, but he was super-careful, hyperconcerned with prices, costs, and he was surprised and somewhat annoyed by her ignorance of these things.

"It's not that I don't care what things cost," she tried to explain. "It's just that I get confused. I'm not good with numbers."

She tried going to bed with him a few more times, deeply knowing this to be a mistake but saying to herself that this time it might work; she might feel the pleasure she pretended (and she knew her pretense to be a serious error, politically incorrect). But, because of what he referred to as his "problem," Lucretia found it hard to put him off entirely; she understood how much his pride was involved, and she was reluctant to hurt that pride, and his feelings.

When he said, as he sometimes gloomily did, that if they broke up she would be the last woman in his life, she also understood that this had less to do with the great love that he professed for her than with his secret, his "problem." Lucretia, the only person privy to that secret, had to be the last in line.

In the women's shelter Lucretia felt herself stretched between extreme emotions: between pity and fear, admiration, sometimes disgust. And occasionally sheer boredom: encouraged by her questions, some of these women would have talked for hours, not always coherently. But many of them were coherent, many interesting, some even funny. A marvelous elderly black woman—from Montana, of all places. A shriveled Mexican-Jewish woman from L.A., with raucous, horrifying tales of endless boyfriends.

Lucretia's story in four installments ran in the Sunday paper, and most of her friends called to say how good it was, congratulations. Edwin, the editor and her old friend (the donor of the white-framed mirror), was highly pleased. Lucretia noted with interest that Burt was among those who did not call.

But Simon did call. Simon Coyne, at that time a voice from her remote past, from Jim and Cambridge days, law school. Although Simon had not been in law school. Eccentrically, everyone felt at the time, he was getting his doctorate in philosophy. Lucretia had heard that he married a Boston girl, and that broke up, and he married someone else. He taught in several small schools around the South. She had not really heard of him for years now, although when he called she realized that he had remained a romantic image in her mind: so tall and fair, with his pipe and tweeds and slightly odd way of speech. He was from Toronto, originally, Lucretia remembered, but he seemed rather "English" than Canadian. More distant than Canadians generally were. More impeccably, remotely courteous.

He was teaching in Berkeley now, Simon said, and yes, he liked it very much. He had found a nice house up on Euclid. His cats liked it, too; he had three. No, he was not married, but two of his three sons were living close by, as it happened.

Why didn't you call me before? Lucretia wanted to ask him. And, When can we see each other? Are you busy tonight? But she managed simply to say, "I'd love to see you; could you come over for supper sometime soon?"

He was terribly busy, as he was sure that she was, too, and besides, he insisted on taking her out to dinner. He would call.

And then she didn't hear from him for a couple of weeks, during which she saw Burt more than she had meant to. She did manage at last to say, "Look, Burt, we can have dinner sometimes if you'd like to, but we can't, uh, go to bed."

His whole face tightened. "I can hardly blame you for that. With my problem."

"It's not that. Honestly." And honestly it was not, not his impotence but his whole severe, self-centered, somewhat hostile character. She would have liked to say, I just don't like you very much, but she said instead, "My heart just isn't in it. I'm sorry."

She should have been rewarded, Lucretia believed, by a phone call from Simon, asking her out to dinner at last. But she was not. Burt called several times, still wanting to see her, and each time the phone rang she imagined that it would be Simon, but it was not. After some time of this she thought, I am much too old to wait for phone calls. And so she called him.

As she had more or less known that he would be, Simon was gallantly contrite. He had meant to call her, he had looked forward to seeing her, but had been stuck with crazy busyness. Department politics, plus high-level university trouble.

She reassured him. Perfectly all right—she had been busy, too. She invited him to dinner.

Oh, no, he said, they must go out, and he named a place that he wanted to try. On the waterfront. Supposed to be excellent food, and also attractive. Hard to get reservations, but he would try, and call her back. They settled on a night. He did call back, to say that he could get a table only at seven, too early, but worth a try. He would pick her up at six-thirty; he would very much look forward to seeing her.

Like a nervous girl, Lucretia wondered what to wear. She was tempted to buy something new and wonderful, but she did not like the styles of that year. She settled on her best old black dress that everyone liked.

At about six her phone rang, and Lucretia's heart sank as she thought, It must be Burt, or worse, it's Simon, canceling.

It was Simon, not canceling but apologizing: A meeting was holding him up, could they possibly meet at the restaurant?

Driving down Broadway, through all the mess of lights and traffic, it occurred to Lucretia that she should have taken a cab; this way they would have to part publicly in some parking lot.

The restaurant was in an old wharf building, remodeled: low, dark ceilings, low lights, a long, rich bar and spectacular view of the bay and the Bay Bridge, Oakland. Black water and huge, dim, looming boats.

At first, coming in, Lucretia could not see Simon, but then she said his name, and she was directed: there, he could have been no one else—tall, lean, fair Simon, with his narrow face, long nose, sardonic mouth. He was standing, smiling, and then coming toward her, hands outstretched to her.

They both said, "Oh, I'm so glad—" and stopped, and laughed.

Their dinner was much in that key, enthusiastically friendly, with good laughs. And relatively impersonal. Simon gracefully deflected anything verging on the personal, did not discuss his two marriages. Instantly sensitive to his mood and needs (this was one of her major skills), Lucretia was amusing. She told funny stories about the paper, about people she had inter-viewed. And they exchanged travel notes; they both loved the South of France, the North of Italy, and they laughed at the unoriginality of their tastes.

Simon's hair, though still thick, was actually white, not blond, as Lucretia had remembered. But, as she sat with him there, she was seeing not the elderly man whom another person might have described as distinguished but rather a young, blond, athletic Simon, with his fair hair and dark-brown eyes, his high, white intellectual brow, and his clever, sensual mouth. She was seeing and responding to a very young man, but also to an aging man, with white hair, whom she hardly knew. With whom she had an animated, no-depth conversation. But to whom she re-sponded, deeply.

As she had imagined, and feared, they parted at her car,

though, bending down to her, Simon asked anxiously, "Should I follow you home? See that you get there safely?"

"Oh no, I drive around all the time. I'll be fine."

A brush of mouths on cheeks. Good night.

Lucretia *knew* that she was much too old to wait for the phone to ring, and yet the next day, a Saturday, she found that that was what she was doing. Despite the fact that her answering machine was functioning, she kept herself within range of her telephone, postponing the small weekend tasks that would make enough noise to drown it out. Postponing neighborhood errands.

Until she thought, This is absolutely, utterly ridiculous. And she went out for an extended walk, doing errands, and even appreciating the beautiful day.

Coming home, though, and noting her machine's nonflashing light, no messages, she experienced a sinking of her spirits: he had not called.

This was crazy, she knew that; she thought, I cannot let myself do this. I will simply have to take charge. I'll call him. This is the nineties, no matter how old we are.

"Simon, it's Lucretia. I just wanted to thank you for dinner. It was really terrific. I had a marvelous time, so lovely to see you, really. I wondered, could you come here for dinner, do you think? Maybe next Friday? Well, actually Saturday's fine. Even better. Great! See you then."

Rack of lamb? Steak *au poivre*? Or were those too show-offy, obvious? Maybe just cracked crab and a salad? But that showed off nothing at all, no cooking. And then she thought, Dear God, it doesn't matter. I'll make something good. Whatever.

But she spent the next week in elaborate fantasies of the possible evening with Simon. In which, sometimes, they went from passionate kissing at the door directly to bed, where things went well.

So obsessed was she that she wondered, Have I fallen in love with Simon? At my age? Is that what this is all about?

She noted that in her dreams several other men appeared whom she had not thought of for years. She dreamed of Jim and of Tommy, of poor dead Jason, of beautiful Silvio. And of several others.

By the actual night on which the actual Simon came to her house for dinner, Lucretia was exhausted, emotionally, so drained that preparing the rack of lamb, God knows an easy dish, had taken great effort. Not to mention blow-drying her hair, brushing it.

It was partly from fatigue, then, that later, in her pretty living room, a familiar and perfect backdrop for love, Lucretia found herself regarding Simon with the most terrible sadness. She was not in love with Simon, she really was not—although he was perfectly nice and in his way quite handsome, still, and interesting. It was simply that he reminded her of love. Some hint of all the men she had ever loved was in his aura, like a scent. One sniff of it and she thought, Ah, love!

That knowledge, or insight, though sad, was relaxing to Lucretia, and she said, "I hope you won't mind if we eat unfashionably early? I'm sort of tired."

"Not at all. It's a terrible thing about age," he said, with his attractive, crooked smile. "I find that I'm tired a lot."

"Oh, I am, too!" and she flashed her answering bright smile, as she thought, Oh good, I won't have to pretend anymore. And I won't even think about falling in love.

But of course she did.

A Very Nice Dog

A few weeks ago, somewhat against my better judgment, I went to a Sunday-lunch party in Sausalito, at which I was deeply bored by the guest of honor, an actor whom I had not especially wanted to meet, and at which I ate very little lunch. But where I met a very nice black dog, an aging Lab, slightly grizzled around the jaw, with large, kind, gentle, and hopeful dark-brown eyes. There he was, lying out in the sun in a corner of my friend Patrick's deck, in the ravishingly beautiful and warm late-October sunlight.

Patrick and I are old, old friends; a very long time ago we were undergraduates together, in Charlottesville, and now we like to say (sometimes we like it) that we are aging together, transported out here to California. I live by myself in San Francisco, and Patrick lives with his friend Oliver in the dark-shingled old Sausalito house, with its newly added cantilevered deck, and its stunning view of the bay and boats, and Alcatraz and Belvedere.

Because of Oliver's allergies they have no pets, although before Oliver entered his life Patrick had Burmese cats, and sometimes a handsome poodle as well. I have three cats. This new dog was not Patrick's, then. "He lives across the street,"

Oliver explained, when I asked, surprised at finding a dog there. That day Oliver was serving, since Patrick had chosen to cook, and they both seemed a little harassed by this change of roles, Oliver being the better and more usual cook. They had little patience for pet conversations—at first.

Patrick is an architect, talented and energetic when he has a project going, depressed when he does not. Genuinely witty, often kind, and sometimes mean, he retains friendships with many old clients. And makes new ones: he had just done a house for this actor, Tom Something, in the Napa Valley. He truly loves his friends, all of them, although he is capable of some manipulation, a little mischief. On the lunch-party day he had clearly enjoyed my discomfort when he would not tell me who was stopping by to pick me up; since I don't drive, some friends and especially Patrick insist on arranging my transportation, when I would really rather do it myself; there are buses to Sausalito, and even a cab is not all that expensive.

At this point I must go back and introduce an element new to this story: a man whom for quite a while I had wanted to know. Just that: he looked interesting, and the little I knew of him was appealing. The appeal was not sexy; he looked to be at least ten years older than I am, and I am too old to be turned on by older men. We had met at some large gathering or other, some time ago, and now when our paths literally crossed on city walks—we both are walkers, we live in the same neighborhood— we would exchange a few words. But he gave an impression of chosen solitude, of great reserve. Justin Solomon, a small dark man with a shock of white hair, and a very slight limp, although he still walked even faster than I did, and I walk fast. He had been a civil rights lawyer, not flamboyant but quietly, wisely effective, and was rumored to give most of his money, earned and inherited from a family brokerage, to those causes. His wife of many years had recently died; she had been a distant friend-connection of Patrick's; thus Patrick knew Justin much better than I did. I thought Justin looked lonely, as well as wryly intelligent—and too thin.

It seems to me simpleminded to label all nurturing impulses "maternal," especially in this instance, but I do like to cook, and I would have liked to ask Mr. Solomon to dinner. However, I felt that I didn't know him well enough, and there is always the female dread (still!) of being misinterpreted, of being perceived as predatory, a sexual aggressor. Or just as lonely.

But since Patrick had this Justin Solomon connection, when he asked me for lunch and began to go on about drivers, I thought, and then said, "What about Justin Solomon?"

"Oh! Well! I hadn't exactly planned to invite dear Justin, it's not exactly his kind of party, but I'll think about it."

"You'll let me know?"

"Of course." He laughed. "Or I may leave it to be a surprise. I'll surprise you with a driver." He laughed again. "I'll send a stretch limo."

The neurotic truth is that I don't much like surprises. I like to know pretty clearly what's going to happen. A kind A.A. friend tells me that this comes from having had alcoholic parents, but I did not want to get into any of that with Patrick. Also, I really thought it likely that he would ask Justin, and had only wanted to tease me.

In the interval between that phone call and the Sunday of the lunch, I had many fantasy conversations with my new best friend, Justin Solomon, as we drove from my house, on Green Street, to Patrick's, in Sausalito. In the course of these talks just possibly he could point to some spot of hope in what I saw as the hopeless awfulness of most recent events, in Russia and Bosnia, in Africa. In Washington, and even L.A.

But as a terrible corrective to this intimate fantasy, I thought too about the stereotype that I feared, of the eager, elderly woman, and I cringed. There must be a lot of such ladies "after" Justin, I thought.

And so I was rather torn about the prospect of my drive to Sausalito, with whomever, and I gave it far too much thought.

What actually happened was that Patrick's friend Oliver picked me up; he had to get some special bread for the lunch at a delicatessen down on Chestnut Street, and so he combined the two errands, me and the special Italian bread.

I was deeply disappointed. I tried not to think about it, or to show it.

Which brings me back to the lunch, the boring too-young actor, Tom, and the nice dog over in the corner of the deck, near the still-flowering azalea.

"Venice is like, like really beautiful," said Tom, as I thought, It's not *like* beautiful, you silly jerk. It *is*.

Tom is very handsome, I guess, with a round blond unlined and (to me) entirely uninteresting, unsexy face, and a deep insistent voice. "Then we did a shoot in Dubrovnik," he said, intoning. "A tragic city—" (At least he did not say it was like a tragic city.)

Many years of practice have enabled me to smile at what I believe and hope are appropriate pauses, though with this Tom it hardly mattered, so concerned was he with his speech, so little aware of his victim-audience. Unless, as I have sometimes suspected of considerable bores, he was doing it on purpose; having sensed my perhaps unusual failure to respond to his charm, he set out to bore me to death.

The lunch was not very good, although Patrick's intentions were generous; gray, overdone slices of cold lamb, and underdone potato salad. Patrick, a somewhat competitive person, does not like to admit that Oliver is the better cook. (Earlier I had even wondered if some misplaced competitiveness with Justin for my friendship had made Patrick not invite Justin to this party.)

I looked over at the dog, who was looking wistfully in the direction of the party, the people, I thought. I also thought how polite of him not to come over and beg for food. And then, as though acknowledging my thought, he turned his head away, showing a profile that was both proud and noble.

"But hey! I really love those guys!" said Tom the actor. Serbs? Bosnians? Venetians? No matter, he was now talking to someone else, and I no longer had to pretend that I was listening.

Very carefully and (I hoped) unobtrusively, then, I packed all my lamb into my napkin, and as though heading into the house I got up and went over to the dog. I knelt beside him and began to feed him the nice cold meat, whose toughness he did not seem to mind. He took every piece very tidily from my hand, with no slobber or visible greed. He looked at me with his beautiful dark-brown–purple velvet eyes, and I felt that an important connection between us had been established.

After maybe five minutes I went back to my table, and the party continued much as before.

And later Oliver took me home at a reasonably early hour, although I could happily have left even earlier. I did not see the dog around as I left.

The next day I called Patrick to thank him for the lunch, and I also said, "What a nice dog that was; I really liked him."

And Patrick said, "Oh, that's Max. Poor baby, he is. Terribly nice, and his people have deserted him. Moved back into town, except on weekends."

"Couldn't you and Oliver adopt him?"

"Well, *I'd* love to. But you know, Oliver's allergies. And the poor dog's so lonesome, he howls all night."

That wrenched my heart; I truly could not bear it. Lonesome Max at night. And although I do have three cats, one of whom is skittish to a point of near psychosis, I was thinking that maybe I could take Max. Emma was already so crazy; she would just have to cope, as the rest of us do.

But at that moment a small and vivid memory filled my

mind: on a recent walk in Cow Hollow, where Justin Solomon and I both live, I had come upon him on Jackson Street, near Alta Plaza park. In his old brown sweater and chinos, Justin did not look like a lawyer, even retired. Together for a few moments that day, we observed the frisking dogs whose recreational terrain that park is, and Justin sighed as he said, "I should get a dog. I'd really like one, but I don't seem to get around to it."

Excitedly I now told Patrick, "Listen! Justin Solomon wants a dog; he told me. You know him. Call him and tell him about Max. Max would be perfect for Justin, they're both so polite."

As I might have known he would, Patrick saw this as a less than wonderful idea. "In the first place," he told me, "the Fowlers probably have their own idea for Max. They may have left him there on purpose. To guard the house."

That seemed a reasonable point, although I argued, "But couldn't you call them? Say that Max is keeping you awake?"

That last was inspired; Patrick likes to complain. A legitimate gripe makes him very happy.

I was right. Patrick agreed to call the Fowlers.

"And if that doesn't work you could call the SPCA," I suggested.

But, hanging up, I felt a little glum as to the possible outcomes of my interference, although at that point I saw my motives as pure. Very likely nothing good would come of this, and I could have made things worse for Max if the SPCA got into it; they might haul him off to a shelter. I considered taking a cab to Sausalito, somehow finding Max and luring him into the car. Taking him home, and even sedating Emma.

Typically, Patrick did not call for several days, during which I had more bad, sad thoughts about lonely Max, howling in Sausalito.

And then Patrick called, and he asked me, "Are you sitting down? I have some really, truly great news."

Well, he did. He had called the Fowlers, and Mrs. Fowler, who turned out to be nice but a little silly, told Patrick that she was so sorry, she too was sad over Max. But they had to be in town most nights. If only they could find a nice home for Max, who was no longer young; he was six, she said. Patrick said he would try to help; he was sorry that his friend was so allergic. And then he actually called Justin Solomon and said that he had heard ("I didn't think you'd want me to say it was you") that Justin might want a dog. And ("this is the part you won't believe") Justin just happened to have an errand in Marin County *that very day*; and Justin came over and met Max and *took him home*. "On approval, he said," said Patrick. "But I could tell that he was in love."

"Patrick, that's really the best story I ever heard." And it was, a totally satisfying story, marvelous: lonely nice Max in a good kind home, and lonely Justin with a very nice dog.

The only missing element for me, and I had to admit this to myself, was my own role. I actually would have liked it if Patrick had given me the proper credit, of course I would. Better to be thought a little indiscreet than to remain almost invisible, I thought.

In fantasy, then, I saw myself again running into Justin—and Max!—somewhere in the neighborhood. It was too much to expect that Max would remember me, despite all the lamb, but I would certainly know him, and his name. And in greeting Max I could explain to Justin how it all came about. Taking full credit.

But would that necessarily lead to our becoming friends? Might not Justin, a somewhat formal man, simply say, "How very kind of you to have thought of me." So that we would continue as before, acquaintances who rarely saw each other, and then only by chance.

What I probably needed, I thought a little sadly, was a dog

of my own. A really nice dog, with beautiful eyes. Like Max. Even Emma would get used to him in time, probably. The one needing a dog is me.

More immediately, though, I could telephone Justin Solomon? Identifying myself, I could include knowing Patrick. I could tell him about the lunch, the lamb. Me and Max. "I'd really love to see him again," I could say. "Should we meet for a walk, or something?"

That seems the best plan, and that is what I will do tomorrow, if not sooner. And then, in the course of the walk, I'll invite him to dinner, and I'll cook something good, with bones—for Max.

The Visit

"She's just dying to see you, so excited, and you really can't refuse a ninety-two-year-old," said Miles Henry to his old friend Grace Lafferty, the famous actress, who was just passing through town, a very quick visit. Miles and Grace were getting on too, but they were nowhere near the awesome age of ninety-two, the age of Miss Louise Dabney, she who was so very anxious to see Grace, "if only for a minute, over tea."

"I really don't remember her awfully well," Grace told Miles. "She was very pretty? But all Mother's friends were pretty. Which made her look even worse. Miles, do we really have to come for tea?"

"You really do." He laughed, as she had laughed, but they both understood what was meant. She and the friend whom she had brought along—Jonathan Hedding, a lawyer, retired, very tall and a total enigma to everyone, so far—must come to tea. As payment, really, for how well Miles had managed their visit: no parties, no pictures or interviews. He had been wonderfully firm, and since he and Grace had been friends forever, if somewhat mysteriously, it was conceded that he had a right to take charge. No one in town would have thought of challenging Miles; for one thing, he was too elusive.

The town was a fairly small one, in the Georgia hill country, not far from Atlanta—and almost everyone there was somewhat excited, interested in this visit; those who were not were simply too young to know who Grace Lafferty was, although their parents had told them: the very famous Broadway actress, then movie star, then occasional TV parts. Grace, who had been born and raised in this town, had barely been back at all. Just briefly, twice, for the funerals of her parents, and one other time when a movie was opening in Atlanta. And now she was here for this very short visit. Nothing to do with publicity or promotions; according to Miles she just wanted to see it all again, and she had carefully picked this season, April, the first weeks of spring, as being the most beautiful that she remembered. Anywhere.

It was odd how she and Miles had stayed friends all these years. One rumor held that they had been lovers very long ago, in the time of Grace's turbulent girlhood, before she got so beautiful (dyed her hair blond) and famous. Miles had been studying architecture in Atlanta then, and certainly they had known each other, but the exact nature of their connection was a mystery, and Miles was far too old-time gentlemanly for anyone to ask. Any more than they would have asked about his two marriages, when he was living up North, and his daughter, whom he never seemed to see.

If Grace's later life from a distance had seemed blessed with fortune (although, four marriages, no children?), one had to admit that her early days were not; her parents, both of them, were difficult. Her father, a classic *beau* of his time, was handsome, and drank too much, and chased girls. Her mother, later also given to drink, was smart and snobbish (she was from South Carolina, and considered Georgia a considerable comedown). She tended to say exactly what she thought, and she wasn't one bit pretty. Neither one of them seemed like ordinary parents, a fact they made a point of—of being above and beyond most normal parental concerns, of not acting like "parents." "We appreciate Grace as a person, and not just because she's our daughter," Hortense, the mother, was fairly often heard to say, which may have accounted for the fact that Grace was a rather unchildlike child: precocious, impertinent, too smart for her own good. Rebellious, always. Unfairly, probably, no one cared a lot for poor wronged Hortense, and almost everyone liked handsome bad Buck Lafferty. Half the women in town had real big, serious crushes on him.

Certainly they made a striking threesome, tall Grace and those two tall men, during the short days of her visit, as they walked slowly, with a certain majesty, around the town. Grace's new friend, or whatever he was, Jonathan Hedding, the lawyer, was the tallest, with heavy, thick gray hair, worn a trifle long for these parts but still, enviably all his own. Miles and Grace were almost the exact same height, she in those heels she always wore, and in the new spring sunlight their hair seemed about the same color, his shining white, hers the palest blond. Grace wore the largest dark glasses that anyone had ever seen—in that way only did she look like a movie star; that and the hair, otherwise she was just tall and a little plump, and a good fifteen years older than she looked to be.

Several times in the course of that walking around Miles asked her, "But was there something particular you wanted to see? I could take you—"

"Oh no." Her throaty voice hesitated. "Oh no, I just wanted to see—everything. The way we're doing. And of course I wanted Jon to see it too."

Miles asked her, "How about the cemetery? These days I know more people there than I do downtown."

She laughed, but she told him, "Oh, great. Let's do go and see the cemetery."

Certainly Grace had been right about the season. The dogwood was just in bloom, white fountains spraying out against the darker evergreens, and fragrant white or lavender wisteria, across the roofs of porches, over garden trellises. Jonquils and narcissus, in their tidy plots, bricked off from the flowing lawns. As Grace several times remarked, the air simply smelled of April. There was nothing like it, anywhere.

"You should come back more often," Miles chided.

"I'm not sure I could stand it." She laughed, very lightly.

The cemetery was old, pre–Civil War; many of the stones were broken, worn, the inscriptions illegible. But there were new ones too, that both Grace and Miles recognized, and remarked upon.

"Look at those Sloanes, they were always the tackiest people. Oh, the Berryhills, they must have struck it rich. And the Calvins, discreet and tasteful as always. Lord, how could there be so many Strouds?"

It was Jonathan who finally said, "Now I see the point of cemeteries. Future entertainment."

They all laughed. It was perhaps the high point of their afternoon, the moment at which they all liked each other best.

And then Grace pointed ahead of them, and she said, "Well for God's sake, there they are. Why did I think I could miss them, totally?"

An imposing granite stone announced LAFFERTY, and underneath, in more discreet lettering, Hortense and Thomas. With dates.

Grace shuddered. "Well, they won't get me in there. Not with them. I'm going to be cremated and have the ashes scattered off Malibu. Or maybe in Central Park."

Five o'clock. Already they were a little late. It was time to go for tea, or rather to be there. Grace had taken even longer than usual with makeup, with general fussing, though Jonathan had reminded her, "At ninety-two she may not see too well, you know."

"Nevertheless." But she hadn't laughed.

Miles lived in a small house just across the street from Miss Dabney's much larger, grander house. It was thus that they knew each other. As Grace and Jonathan drove up he was out in front poking at leaves, but actually just waiting for them, as they all knew.

"I'm sorry—" Grace began.

"It's all right, but whyever are you so nerved up?"

"Oh, I don't know—"

Inside Miss Dabney's entrance hall, to which they had been admitted by a white-aproned, very small black woman, where they were told to wait, Jonathan tried to exchange a complicitous look with Grace: after all, she was with him. But she seemed abstracted, apart.

The parlor into which they were at last led by the same small silent maid was predictably crowded—with tiny tables and chairs, with silver frames and photographs, loveseats and glassed-in bookcases. And, in the center of it all, Miss Dabney herself, yellowed white hair swathed about her head like a bandage but held up stiff and high, as though the heavy pearl choker that she wore were a splint. Her eyes, shining out through folds of flesh, were tiny and black, and brilliant. She held out a gnarled, much-jeweled hand to Grace (was Grace supposed to kiss the rings? She did not). The two women touched fingers.

When Miss Dabney spoke her voice was amazingly clear, rather high, a little hoarse but distinct. "Grace Lafferty, you do look absolutely lovely," she said. "I'd know you anywhere; in a way you haven't changed a bit."

"Oh well, but you look—" Grace started to say.

"Now now. I'm much too old to be flattered. That's how come I don't have handsome men around me anymore." Her glance flicked out to take in Miles, and then Jonathan. "But of course no man was ever as handsome as your daddy."

"No, I guess—"

"Too bad your mother wasn't pretty too. I think it would have improved her character."

"Probably—"

Miss Dabney leaned forward. "You know, we've always been so proud of you in this town. Just as proud as proud."

The effect of this on Grace was instant; something within her settled down, some set of nerves, perhaps. She almost relaxed. Miles with relief observed this, and Jonathan too.

"Yes, indeed we have. For so many, many things," Miss Dabney continued.

A warm and pleasant small moment ensued, during which in an almost preening way Grace glanced at Jonathan—before Miss Dabney took it up again.

"But do you know what you did that made us the very proudest of all?" Quite apparently wanting no answer, had one been possible, she seemed to savor the expectation her non-question had aroused.

"It was many, many years ago, and your parents were giving a dinner party," she began—as Miles thought, Oh dear God, oh Jesus.

"And you were just this adorable little two- or three-year-old. And somehow you got out of your crib and you came downstairs, and you crawled right under the big white linen tablecloth, it must have seemed like a circus tent to you—and you bit your mother right there on the ankle. Good and hard! She jumped and cried out, and Buck lifted up the tablecloth and there you were. I don't remember quite how they punished you, but we all just laughed and laughed. Hortense was not the most popular lady in town, and I reckon one time or another we'd all had an urge to bite her. And you did it! We were all just so proud!"

"But—" Grace protests, or rather, she begins to protest. She seems then, though, to remember certain rules. One held that

Southern ladies did not contradict other ladies, especially if the other one is very old. She also remembered a rule from her training as an actress: you do not exhibit uncontrolled emotion of your own.

Grace simply says, "It's funny, I don't remember that at all," and she smiles, beautifully.

Miles, though, who has known her for so very long, and who has always loved her, for the first time fully understands just what led her to become an actress, and also why she is so very good at what she does.

"Well of course you don't," Miss Dabney is saying. "You were much too young. But it's a wonder no one ever told you, considering how famous—how famous that story was."

Jonathan, who feels that Grace is really too old for him, but whose fame he has enjoyed, up to a point, now tells Miss Dabney, "It's a marvelous story. You really should write it, I think. Some magazine—"

Grace gives him the smallest but most decisive frown—as Miles, watching, thinks, Oh, good.

And Grace now says, abandoning all rules, "I guess up to now no one ever told me so as not to make me feel small and bad. I guess they knew I'd have to get very old and really mean before I'd think that was funny."

As Miles thinks, Ah, that's my girl!

The Last Lovely City

Old and famous, an acknowledged success both in this country and in his native Mexico, though now a sadhearted widower, Dr. Benito Zamora slowly and unskillfully navigates the high, sharp curves on the road to Stinson Beach, California—his destination. From time to time, barely moving his heavy, white-maned head, he glances at the unfamiliar young woman near him on the seat—the streaky-haired, underweight woman in a very short skirt and green sandals (her name is Carla) who has somewhat inexplicably invited him to come along to this party. What old hands, Benito thinks, of his own, on the wheel, an old beggar's hands. What can this girl want of me? he wonders. Some new heaviness around the doctor's neck and chin makes him look both strong and fierce, and his deep-set black eyes are powerful, still, and unrelenting in their judgmental gaze, beneath thick, uneven, white brows.

"We're almost there," he tells the girl, this Carla.

"I don't care; I love the drive," she says, and moves her head closer to the window, so her long hair fans out across her shoulders. "Do you go back to Mexico very often?" she turns now to ask him.

"Fairly. My very old mother still lives there. Near Oaxaca."

"Oh, I've been to Oaxaca. So beautiful." She beams. "The hotel—"

"My mother's not in the Presidente."

She grins, showing small, white, even teeth. "Well, you're right. I did stay there. But it is a very nice hotel."

"Very nice," he agrees, not looking at her.

His mother is not the doctor's only reason for going to Oaxaca. His interests are actually in almost adjacent Chiapas, where he oversees and has largely funded two large free clinics—hence his fame, and his nickname, Dr. Do-Good (to Benito, an epithet replete with irony, and one that he much dislikes).

They have now emerged from the dark, tall, covering woods, the groves of redwood, eucalyptus, occasional laurel, and they are circling down the western slope as the two-lane road forms wide arcs. Ahead of them is the sea, the white curve of beach, and strung-out Stinson, the strange, small coastal town of rich retirees; weekenders, also rich; and a core population of former hippies, now just plain poor, middle-aged people with too many children. In his palmier days, his early, successful years, Dr. Zamora often came to Stinson from San Francisco on Sundays for lunch parties, first as a semi-sought-after bachelor ("But would you want your daughter actually to marry . . . ?" Benito thought he felt this question), and later, less often, with his bride, the fairest of them all, his wife, his lovely blond. His white soul. Elizabeth.

After Elizabeth died, now some five months ago, in April, friends and colleagues were predictably kind—many invitations, too many solicitous phone calls. And then, just as predictably (he had seen this happen with relatives of patients), all the attention fell off, and he was often alone. And at a time impossible for trips to Mexico: rains made most of the roads in Chiapas impassable, and he feared that he was now too old for the summer heat. Besides, these days the clinics actually ran quite well without him; he imagined that all they really needed was the money that came regularly from his banks. (Had that always been the case? he wondered. Were all those trips to Chiapas unnecessary, ultimately self-serving?) And his mother, in her tiny stucco villa, near Oaxaca, hardly recognized her oldest living son.

Too much time alone, then, and although he had always known that would happen, was even in a sense prepared, the doctor is sometimes angry: Why must they leave him now, when he is so vulnerable? Is no one able to imagine the daily lack, the loss with which he lives?

And then this girl, this Carla, whom the doctor had met at a dinner a month or so before, called and asked him to the lunch, at Stinson Beach. "I hope you don't mind a sort of last-minute invitation," she said, "but I really loved our talk, and I wanted to see you again, and this seemed a good excuse." He gratefully accepted, although he remembered very little of her, really, except for her hair, which was very long and silky-looking, streaked all shades of brown, with yellow. He remembered her hair, and that she seemed nice, a little shy; she was quiet, and so he had talked too much. ("Not too unusual, my darling," Elizabeth might have said.) He thinks she said she worked for a newspaper; it now seems too late to ask. He believes she is intelligent, and serious. Curious about his clinics.

But in the short interval between her call and this drive a host of fantasies has crowded old Benito's imagination. She looked about thirty, this girl did, but these days most women look young; she could be forty-two. Still a long way from his own age, but such things did happen. One read of them.

Or was it possible that Carla meant to write about him for her paper? The doctor had refused most interviews for years; had refused until he noticed that no one had asked, not for years.

"What did you say the name of our hostess was?" he thinks to ask her as they round the last curve and approach the first buildings of the town.

"Posey Pendergast. You've never met her?"

"I don't think so, but the name—something goes off in my head."

"Everyone knows Posey; I really thought you would. She's quite marvelous."

"Quite marvelous" is a phrase that Benito (Elizabeth used to agree) finds cautionary; those marvelous people are almost as bad as "characters." All those groups he is sure not to like, how they do proliferate, thinks old Benito sourly, aware of the cruel absence of Elizabeth, with her light laugh, agreeing.

"I'm sure you'll know some of her friends," adds Carla.

Posey Pendergast is a skinny old wreck of a woman, in a tattered straw sun hat and a red, Persian-looking outfit. She breathes heavily. Emphysema and some problems with her heart, the doctor thinks, automatically noting the pink-white skin, faintly bluish mouth, and arthritic hands—hugely blue-veined, rings buried in finger flesh. "I've been hearing of you for years," she tells Benito in her raspy, classy voice. Is she English? No, more like Boston, or somewhere back there, the doctor decides. She goes on. "I can't believe we've never met. I'm *so* glad Carla brought you."

"This is some house," he says solemnly (using what Elizabeth called his innocent-Indian pose, which is one of his tricks).

It is some house, and the doctor now remembers walking past it, with Elizabeth, marveling at its size and opulence. It was right out there on the beach, not farther along in Seadrift, with the other big, expensive houses, but out in public—a huge house built up on pilings, all enormous beams, and steel and glass, and diagonal boards.

"My son designed it for me," Posey Pendergast is saying. "Carla's friend," she adds, just as some remote flash is going off in the doctor's mind: he used to hear a lot about this Posey, he recalls, something odd and somewhat scandalous, but from whom? Not Elizabeth, he is sure of that, although she was fond of gossip and used to lament his refusal to talk about patients. Did he hear of Posey from some patient? Some old friend?

This large room facing the sea is now fairly full of people. Women in short, silk, flowered dresses or pastel pants, men in linen or cashmere coats. Rich old gringos is Benito's instant assessment. He notes what seems an unusual number of hearing aids.

He and Carla are introduced around by Posey, although Carla seems already to know a number of the guests. People extend their hands; they all say how nice it is to meet the doctor; several people say that they have heard so much about him. And then, from that roster of Anglo-Saxon names, all sounding somewhat alike, from those voices, nasal Eastern to neutral Californian, Benito hears a familiar sound: "Oh." (It is the drawn-out "Oh" that he recognizes.) "Oh, but I've known Dr. Zamora *very* well, for a *very* long time."

He is confronted by an immense (she must weigh two hundred pounds) short woman, with a huge puff of orange hair, green eyeshadow, and the pinkish spots that skin cancer leaves marking her pale, lined forehead. It is Dolores. Originally Dolores Gutierrez—then Osborne, then Graham, and then he lost track. But here she is before him, her doughy face tightened into a mask, behind which he can indistinctly see the beauty that she was.

"Benito Zamora. Benny Zamora. What an absolutely awful name, my darling. So *spic*," said Dolores, almost fifty years ago.

"How about Dolores Gutierrez?"

"I can marry out of it, and I certainly plan to. Why else would I even think of Boy Osborne, or for that matter Whitney Satterfield? But you, you simply have to change *yours*. How about Benjamin Orland? That keeps some of the sound, you see? I really don't like names to begin with 'Z.' "

"This is an extremely ugly room," he told her.

She laughed. "I know, but poor dear Norman thinks it's the cat's pajamas, and it's costing him a fortune."

"When you laugh I feel ice on my back." He shivered.

"Pull the sheet up. There. My, you are a gorgeous young man. You really are. Too bad about your name. You don't look so terribly spic."

They were in the pink-and-gold suite of a lesser Nob Hill hotel, definitely not the Mark or the Fairmont, but still no doubt costing poor Norman a lot. Heavy, gold-threaded, rose-colored draperies, barely parted, yielded a narrow blue view of the San Francisco Bay, the Bay Bridge, a white slice of Oakland. The bedspread, a darker rose, also gold-threaded, lay in a heavy, crumpled mass on the floor. The sheets were pink, and the shallow buttocks of Dolores Gutierrez were ivory—cool and smooth. Her hair, even then, was false gold.

"You know what I'd really like you to do? Do you want to know?" Her voice was like scented oil, the young doctor thought, light and insidious and finally dirty, making stains.

"I do want to know," he told her.

"Well, this is really perverse. *Really*. It may be a little too much for you." She was suddenly almost breathless with wanting to tell him what she really wanted, what was so terrifically exciting.

"Tell me." His breath caught, too, although in a rational way he believed that they had surely done everything. He stroked her smooth, cool bottom.

"I want you to pay me," she said. "I know you don't have much money, so that will make it all the more exciting. I want you to pay me a lot. And I might give it back to you, but then again I might not."

After several minutes, during which he took back his hand, Benito told her, "I don't want to do that. I don't think it would be fun."

And now this new Dolores, whose laugh is deeper, tells him, "This is a classic situation, isn't it, my angel? Famous man runs into an old lady friend, who's run to fat?" She laughs, and, as before, Benito shivers. "But wherever did you meet my darling old Posey?"

"Just now, actually. I never saw her before."

"The love of my life," Dolores declaims, as the doctor reflects that this could well be true, for he has just remembered a few more lines from their past. "I really don't like men at all," Dolores confided back then. "I only need them, although I'm terrified of them. And now I've fallen in love with this beautiful girl, who is very rich, of course. Even thinner than I am. With the most delicious name. Posey Pendergast. You must meet her one day. She would like you, too."

Wishing no more of this, and wishing no more of Dolores, ever, Benito turns in search of Carla, who seems to have vanished or hidden herself in the crowd that now populates this oversized room, milling around the long bar table and spilling out onto the broad deck that faces the sea. As he catches sight of the deck, the doctor instinctively moves toward it, even as Dolores is saying, "You must come back and tell me how you made all that money, Dr. Do-Good."

"Excuse me," he mutters stiffly, making for the door. He is not at all graceful in the usual way of Latins; Elizabeth said that from time to time.

From the deck San Francisco is still invisible; it lurks there behind the great cliffs of land, across the surging, dark-streaked sea. The tall, pale city, lovely and unreal. Benito thinks of his amazement at that city, years back, when he roamed its streets as an almost indigent medical student—at Stanford, in those days a city medical school, at Clay and Webster Streets, in Pacific Heights. How lonely he used to feel as he walked across those hills and stared at massive apartment houses, at enormous family houses—how isolated and full of greed. He *wanted* the city, both to possess and to immerse himself in it. It is hardly surprising, he now thinks—with a small, wry, private smile—that he ended up in bed with Dolores Gutierrez, and that a few years later he found himself the owner of many sleazy blocks of hotels in the Tenderloin.

But that is not how he ended up, the doctor tells himself, in a fierce interior whisper. He ended up with Elizabeth, who was both beautiful and good, a serious woman, with whom he lived harmoniously, if sometimes sadly (they had no children, and Elizabeth was given to depression), near St. Francis Wood, in a house with a view of everything—the city and the sea, the Farallon Islands.

Nor is that life with Elizabeth how he ended up, actually. The actual is now, of course, and he has ended up alone. Childless and without Elizabeth.

The doctor takes deep breaths, inhaling the cool, fresh wind, and exhaling, he hopes and believes, the germs of self-pity that sometimes enter and threaten to invade his system. He looks back to the great Marin headlands, those steep, sweeping hills of green. Far out at sea he sees two small, hopeful white boats, sails bobbing against the dark horizon.

Looking back inside the house, he sees Carla in intimate-seeming conversation with withered old Posey. Fresh from the intimations of Dolores, he shudders: Posey must be even older than he is, and quite unwell. But before he has time for speculation along those lines, he is jolted by a face, suddenly glimpsed behind the glass doors: bright-eyed and buck-toothed, thinner and grayer but otherwise not much aged, in a starched white embroidered shirt (Why on earth? Does he want to look Mexican?), that lawyer, Herman Tolliver.

"Well, of course they should be condemned; half this town should be condemned, are you crazy?" Tolliver grinned sideways, hiding his teeth. "The point is, they're not going to be condemned. Somebody's going to make a bundle off them. And from where I'm sitting it looks like you could be the guy. Along with me." Another grin, which was then extinguished as Tolliver tended to the lighting of a new cigar.

In that long-ago time (about forty years back) the doctor had just opened his own office and begun his cardiology practice. And had just met a young woman, with straw-blond hair, clear, dark-blue eyes, and a sexy overbite—Carole Lombard with a Gene Tierney mouth. A young woman of class and style, none of which he could ever afford. Elizabeth Montague: her very name was defeating. Whoever would exchange Montague for Zamora?

None of which excused Benito's acquiescence in Tolliver's scheme. (Certain details as to the precise use of Tolliver's "hotels" Benito arranged not quite to know, but he had, of course, his suspicions.) It ended in making the doctor and his wife, Elizabeth Montague Zamora, very rich. And in funding the clinics for the indigent of Chiapas.

After that first encounter with Herman Tolliver, the doctor almost managed never to see him again. They talked on the phone, or, in the later days of success and busyness, through secretaries. Benito was aware of Tolliver, aware that they were both making a great deal of money, but otherwise he was fairly successful in dismissing the man from his mind.

One morning, not long before Elizabeth died, she looked up from the paper at breakfast (Benito only scanned the *New York Times,* did not read local news at all) and said, "Didn't you used to know this scandalous lawyer, this Tolliver?"

"We've met." But how did Elizabeth know that? Benito, shaken, wondered, and then remembered: some time back there had been phone calls, a secretary saying that Mr. Tolliver wanted to get in touch (fortunately, nothing urgent). Just enough to fix the name in Elizabeth's mind. "Is he scandalous?" Benito then asked his wife, very lightly.

"Well, some business with tax evasion. Goodness, do all lawyers do things like that these days?"

Aware of his own relief (he certainly did not want public scandals connected with Tolliver), Benito told her, "I very much doubt it, my darling."

And that was the end of that, it seemed.

Carla is now talking to both old Posey and Herman Tolliver, but the doctor can see from her posture that she doesn't really like Tolliver, does not really want to talk to him. She is barely giving him the time of day, holding her glass out in front of her like a shield, or a weapon. She keeps glancing about, not smiling, as Tolliver goes on talking.

Is she looking for him? the doctor wonders. Does she ask herself what has happened to old Benito? He smiles to himself at this notion—and then, almost at the same moment, is chilled with longing for Elizabeth.

A problem with death, the doctor has more than once thought, is its removal of all the merciful dross of memory: he no longer remembers any petty annoyances, ever, or even moments of boredom, irritation, or sad, failed acts of love. All that is erased, and he only recalls, with the most cruel, searing accuracy, the golden peaks of their time together. Beautiful days, long nights of love. He sees Elizabeth at their dining table, on a rare warm summer night. Her shoulders bare and white; a thin gold necklace that he has brought her from Oaxaca shines in the candlelight; she is bending toward their guest, old Dr. McPherson, from med-school days. Benito sees, too, McPherson's wife, and other colleague guests with their wives—all attractive, pale, and well dressed. But none so attractive as his own wife, his pale Elizabeth.

"Oh, there you are," Carla says, coming up to him suddenly.

"You couldn't see me out here? I could see you quite clearly," he tells her, in his sober, mechanical voice.

"I was busy fending off that creep, Tolliver. Mr. Slime." She tosses her hair, now gleaming in the sunlight. "I can't imagine what Posey sees in him. Do you know him?"

"We've met," the doctor admits. "But how do you know him?"

"I'm a reporter, remember? I meet everyone."

"And Posey Pendergast? You know her because—"

But that question and its possible answer are interrupted, cut off by the enormous, puffing arrival of Dolores. "Oh, here's where you've got to," she tells Benito and Carla, as though she had not seen them from afar and headed directly to where they stand, leaning together against the balcony's railing. "Carla, I'm absolutely in love with your hair," says Dolores.

Carla giggles—out of character for her, the doctor thinks—and then, another surprise, she takes his arm for a moment and laughs as she asks him, "Why don't you ever say such flattering things to me?"

Is she flirting with him, seriously flirting? Well, she could be. Such things do happen, the doctor reminds himself. And she seems a very honest young woman, and kind. She could brighten my life, he thinks, and lighten my home, all those rooms with their splendid views that seem to have darkened.

"Don't you want some lunch?" she is asking. "Can I get you something?"

Before he can answer (and he had very much liked the idea of her bringing him food), Dolores, again interrupting, has stated, "He never eats. Can't you tell? Dr. Abstemious, I used to call him."

"Well, I'm really hungry, I'll see you two later." And with an uncertain smile (from shyness? annoyance? and if annoyance, at which of them?), Carla has left. She is pushing back into the room, through the crowds; she has vanished behind the glass.

Looking at Dolores then, the old doctor is seized with rage; he stares at that puffy, self-adoring face, those dark and infinitely self-pitying eyes. How he longs to push her against the railing, down into the sand! How he despises her!

"My darling, I believe you're really hungry after all," is what Dolores says, but she may have felt some of his anger, for she deftly steps sideways, on her high, thin, dangerous heels, just out of his reach.

"Not in the least," says Benito rigidly. "In fact, I think I'll go for a walk on the beach."

Down on the sand, though, as he walks along the dark, packed strip that is nearest to the sea, Benito's confusion increases. He feels the presence of those people in that rather vulgar, glassed-in house behind him—of Dolores Gutierrez and Herman Tolliver, and God knows who else, what other ghosts from his past whom he simply failed to see. As though they were giants, he feels their looming presences, and feels their connection to some past year or years of his own life. He no longer knows where he is. What place is this, what country? What rolling gray-green ocean does he walk beside? What year it this, and what is his own true age?

Clearly, some derangement has taken hold of him, or nearly, and Benito is forced to fight back with certain heavy and irrefutable facts: this is September, 1990, the last year of a decade, and the year in which Elizabeth died. He is in Stinson Beach, and if he continues walking far enough along the coast—he is heading south, toward the Golden Gate—he will be in sight of beautiful, mystical San Francisco, the city and the center of all his early dreams, the city where everything, finally, happened: Dolores Gutierrez and his medical degree; Herman Tolliver and those hotels. His (at last) successful medical practice. Elizabeth, and all that money, and his house with its fabulous views. His fame as Dr. Do-Good.

His whole San Francisco history seems to rise up then and to break his heart. The city itself is still pale and distant and invisible, and he stands absolutely still, a tall figure on the sand, next to an intricate, crumbling sand castle that some children have recently abandoned.

Hearing running feet behind him, at that moment the doctor turns in fright—expecting what? some dangerous stranger?—but it is Carla, out of breath, her hair streaming backward in the wind. His savior.

"Ah, you," he says to her. "You ran."

"And these are not the greatest running shoes." She laughs, pointing down to her sandals, now sand-streaked and damp.

"You came after me—"

She looks down, and away. "Well. It was partly an excuse to get out of there. It was getting a little claustrophobic, and almost everyone I talked to was hard-of-hearing."

"Oh, right."

"Well, shall we walk for a while?"

"Yes."

Walking along with Carla, the doctor finds that those giants from his dark and tangled past have quite suddenly receded:

Dolores and Tolliver have shrunk down to human size, the size of people accidentally encountered at a party. Such meetings can happen to anyone, easily, especially at a certain age.

Benito even finds that he can talk about them. "To tell you the truth"—an ominous beginning, he knows, but it is what he intends to do—"I did some business with Herman Tolliver a long time ago, maybe forty years. It came out very well, financially, but I'm still a little ashamed of it. It seems to me now that I was pretending to myself not to know certain things that I really did know."

"You mean about his hotels?"

"Well, yes. Hotels. But how do you—does everyone know all that?"

"I'm a reporter, remember? Investigative." She laughs, then sniffles a little in the hard, cold ocean wind. "He had an idea a few years back about running for supervisor, but I'm sure he was really thinking mayor, ultimately. But we dug up some stuff."

"Here, take my handkerchief—"

"Thanks. Anyway, he was persuaded to forget it. There were really ugly things about preteenage Asian girls. We made a bargain: the papers would print only the stuff about his 'tax problems' if he'd bow out." She sighs, a little ruefully. "I don't know. It might have been better to let him get into politics; he might have done less harm that way."

This walk, and the conversation, are serving both to calm and to excite the doctor. Simultaneously. Most peculiar. He feels a calm, and at the same time a strange, warm, quiet excitement. "How do you mean?" he asks Carla.

"Oh, he got in deeper and deeper. Getting richer and richer."

"I got richer and richer, too, back then. Sometimes I felt like I owned the whole goddam city." Benito is paying very little attention to what he is saying; it is now all he can do to prevent himself from speaking his heart, from saying, "When will you marry me? How soon can that be?"

"But that's great that you made so much money," Carla says. "That way you could start those clinics, and do so much good."

Barely listening, Benito murmurs, "I suppose . . ."

She could redecorate the house any way she would like to, he thinks. Throw things out, repaint, reupholster, hang mirrors. His imagination sees, all completed, a brilliant house, with Carla its brilliant, shining center.

"How did you happen to know Dolores?" Carla is asking.

By now they have reached the end of the beach: a high mass of rocks left there by mammoth storms the year before. Impassable. Beyond lies more beach, more cliffs, more headlands, all along the way to the sight of the distant city.

"Actually, Dolores was an old girlfriend, you might say." Since he cares so much for this girl, Benito will never lie to her, he thinks. "You might not believe this, but she was quite a beauty in her day."

"Oh, I believe you. She's still so vain. That hair."

Benito laughs, feeling pleased, and wondering, Can this adorable girl be, even slightly, jealous? "You're right there," he tells Carla. "Very vain, always was. Of course, she's a few years older than I am."

"I guess we have to turn around now," says Carla.

"And now Dolores tells me that she and Posey Pendergast were at one time, uh, lovers," Benito continues, in his honest mode.

"I guess they could have been," Carla muses. "On the other hand, it's my impression that Dolores lies a lot. And Posey I'm just not sure about. Nor any of that group, for that matter. Tolliver, all those people. It's worrying." She laughs. "I guess I sort of hoped you might know something about them. Sort of explain them to me."

Not having listened carefully to much of this, Benito rephrases the question he does not remember having begun to ask before, which Dolores interrupted: "How do you know Posey?" he asks Carla.

"It's mostly her son I know. Patrick. He's my fiancé, I guess you could say. We were planning to make it legal, and I guess we will. Any day now." And she goes on, "Actually, Patrick was supposed to come today, and then he couldn't, and then I thought—I thought of you."

The sun has sunk into the ocean, and Benito's heart has sunk with it, drowned. He shudders, despising himself. How could he possibly have imagined, how not have guessed?

"How nice," Benito remarks, without meaning, and then he babbles on, "You know, the whole city seems so corrupt these days. It's all real estate, and deals."

"Get real," she chides him, in her harsh young voice. "That's what it's like all over."

"Well, I'll be awfully glad to get back to Mexico. At least I more or less understand the corruption there."

"Are you going back for long?"

The wind is really cold now. Benito sniffs, wishing he had his handkerchief back, and unable to ask for it. "Oh, permanently," he tells Carla. "A permanent move. I want to be near my clinics. See how they're doing. Maybe help."

The doctor had no plan to say (much less to do) any of this before he spoke, but he knows that he is now committed to this action. This permanent move. He will buy a house in San Cristóbal de las Casas, and will bring his mother there, from Oaxaca, to live in that house for as long as she lasts. And he, for as long as he lasts, will work in his clinics, with his own poor.

"Well, that's great. Maybe we could work out a little inter-view before you go."

"Well, maybe."

"I wonder if we couldn't just bypass the party for now," says Carla. "I'm just not up to going in again, going through all that, with those people."

"Nor I," the doctor tells her. "Good idea."

"I'll call Posey as soon as we get back. Did she tell you the house was up for sale? She may have sold it today—all those people . . ."

Half hearing her, the doctor is wrestling with the idea of a return to the city, which is suddenly unaccountably terrible to him; he dreads the first pale, romantic view of it from the bridge, and then the drive across town to his empty house, after dropping Carla off on Telegraph Hill. His house with its night views of city hills and lights. But he braces himself with the thought that he won't be in San Francisco long this time. That as soon as he can arrange things he will be back in Chiapas, in Mexico. For the rest of his life.

And thus he manages to walk on, following Carla past the big, fancy house, for sale—and all those people, the house's rich and crazily corrupt population. He manages to walk across the sand toward his car, and the long, circuitous, and risky drive to the city.

The Islands

What does it mean to love an animal, a pet, in my case a cat, in the fierce, entire, and unambivalent way that some of us do? I really want to know this. Does the cat (did the cat) represent some person, a parent, or a child? some part of one's self? I don't think so—and none of the words or phrases that one uses for human connections sounds quite right: "crazy about," "really liked," "very fond of"—none of those describes how I felt and still feel about my cat. Many years ago, soon after we got the cat (her name was Pink), I went to Rome with my husband, Andrew, whom I really liked; I was crazy about Andrew, and very fond of him too. And I have a most vivid memory of lying awake in Rome, in the pretty bed in its deep alcove, in the nice small hotel near the Borghese Gardens—lying there, so fortunate to be in Rome, with Andrew, and missing Pink, a small striped cat with no tail—missing Pink unbearably. Even blaming Andrew for having brought me there, although he loved her too, almost as much as I did. And now Pink has died, and I cannot accept or believe in her death, any more than I could believe in Rome. (Andrew also died, three years ago, but this is not his story.)

A couple of days after Pink died (this has all been recent), I went to Hawaii with a new friend, Slater. It had not been planned that way; I had known for months that Pink was slowly failing (she was nineteen), but I did not expect her to die. She just suddenly did, and then I went off to "the islands," as my old friend Zoe Pinkerton used to call them, in her nasal, mon-eyed voice. I went to Hawaii as planned, which interfered with my proper mourning for Pink. I feel as though those islands interposed themselves between her death and me. When I needed to be alone, to absorb her death, I was over there with Slater.

Slater is a developer; malls and condominium complexes all over the world. Andrew would not have approved of Slater, and sometimes I don't think I do either. Slater is tall and lean, red-haired, a little younger than I am, and very attractive, I suppose, although on first meeting Slater I was not at all drawn to him (which I have come to think is one of the reasons he found me so attractive, calling me the next day, insisting on dinner that night; he was probably used to women who found him terrific, right off). But I thought Slater talked too much about money, or just talked too much, period.

Later on, when I began to like him a little better (I was flat-tered by all that attention, is the truth), I thought that Slater's very differences from Andrew should be a good sign. You're supposed to look for opposites, not reproductions, I read somewhere.

Andrew and I had acquired Pink from Zoe, a very rich alcoholic, at that time new neighbor of ours in Berkeley. Having met Andrew down in his bookstore, she invited us to what turned out to be a very long Sunday-lunch party in her splendidly decked and viewed new Berkeley hills house. Getting to know some of the least offensive neighbors, is how she probably thought of it. Her style was harsh, abrasive; anything for a laugh was surely one of her mottoes, but she was pretty funny, fairly often. We saw her around when she first moved to Berkeley (from Ireland: a brief experiment that had not worked out too well). And then she met Andrew in his store, and found that we were neighbors, and she invited us to her party, and Andrew fell in love with a beautiful cat. "The most beautiful cat I ever saw," he told Zoe, and she was, soft and silver, with great blue eyes. The mother of Pink.

"Well, you're in luck," Zoe told us. "That's Molly Bloom, and she just had five kittens. They're all in a box downstairs, in my bedroom, and you get to choose any one you want. It's your door prize for being such a handsome couple."

Andrew went off to look at the kittens, and then came back up to me. "There's one that's really great," he said. "A tailless wonder. Must be part Manx."

As in several Berkeley hills houses, Zoe's great sprawl of a bedroom was downstairs, with its own narrow deck, its view of the bay and the bridge, and of San Francisco. The room was the most appalling mess I had ever seen. Clothes, papers, books, dirty glasses, spilled powder, more clothes dumped everywhere. I was surprised that my tidy, somewhat censorious husband even entered, and that he was able to find the big wicker basket (filled with what looked to be discarded silk underthings, presumably clean) in which five very tiny kittens mewed and tried to rise and stalk about on thin, uncertain legs.

The one that Andrew had picked was gray striped, a tabby, with a stub of a tail, very large eyes, and tall ears. I agreed that she was darling, how great it would be to have a cat again; our last cat, Lily, who was sweet and pretty but undistinguished, had died some years ago. And so Andrew and I went back upstairs and told Zoe, who was almost very drunk, that we wanted the one with no tail.

"Oh, Stubs," she rasped. "You don't have to take that one.

What are you guys, some kind of Berkeley bleeding hearts? You can have a whole cat." And she laughed, delighted as always with her own wit.

No, we told her. We wanted that particular cat. We liked her best.

Aside from seeing the cats—our first sight of Pink!—the best part of Zoe's lunch was her daughter, Lucy, a shy, pretty, and very gentle young woman—as opposed to the other guests, a rowdy, oil-rich group, old friends of Zoe's from Texas.

"What a curious litter," I remarked to Andrew, walking home up Marin to our considerably smaller house. "All different. Five different patterns of cat."

"Five fathers." Andrew had read a book about this, I could tell. Andrew read everything. "It's called multiple insemination, and occurs fairly often in cats. It's theoretically possible in humans, but they haven't come across any instances." He laughed, really pleased with this lore.

"It's sure something to think about."

"Just don't."

Andrew. An extremely smart, passionate, selfish, and generous man, a medium-successful bookstore owner. A former academic: he left teaching in order to have more time to read, he said. Also (I thought) he much preferred being alone in his store to the company of students or, worse, of other professors— a loner, Andrew. Small and almost handsome, competitive, a gifted tennis player, mediocre pianist. Gray hair and gray-green eyes. As I have said, I was crazy about Andrew (usually). I found him funny and interestingly observant, sexy and smart. His death was more grievous to me than I can (or will) say.

"You guys don't have to take Stubs; you can have a whole cat all your own." Zoe Pinkerton on the phone, a few days later. Like many alcoholics, she tended to repeat herself, although in Zoe's case some vast Texas store of self-confidence may have fueled her repetitions.

And we in our turn repeated: we wanted the little one with no tail.

Zoe told us that she would bring "Stubs" over in a week or so; then the kittens would be old enough to leave Molly Bloom.

Andrew: "Molly Bloom indeed."

I: "No wonder she got multiply inseminated."

Andrew: "Exactly."

We both, though somewhat warily, liked Zoe. Or we were both somewhat charmed by her. For one thing, she made it clear that she thought we were great. For another, she was smart; she had read even more than Andrew had.

A very small woman, she walked with a swagger; her laugh was loud, and liberal. I sometimes felt that Pink was a little like Zoe—a tiny cat with a high, proud walk; a cat with a lot to say.

In a couple of weeks, then, Zoe called, and she came over with this tiny tailless kitten under her arm. A Saturday afternoon. Andrew was at home, puttering in the garden like the good Berkeley husband that he did not intend to be.

Zoe arrived in her purple suede pants and a vivid orange sweater (this picture is a little poignant; fairly soon after that the booze began to get the better of her legs, and she stopped taking walks at all). She held out a tiny kitten, all huge gray eyes and pointed ears. A kitten who took one look at us and began to purr; she purred for several days, it seemed, as she walked all over our house and made it her own. This is absolutely the best place I've ever been, she seemed to say, and you are the greatest people—you are my people.

From the beginning, then, our connection with Pink seemed like a privilege; automatically we accorded her rights that poor Lily would never have aspired to.

She decided to sleep with us. In the middle of the night there came a light soft plop on our bed, which was low and wide, and then a small sound, *mmrrr,* a little announcement of her presence. "Littlest announcer," said Andrew, and we called her that, among her other names. Neither of us ever mentioned locking her out.

Several times in the night she would leave us and then return, each time with the same small sound, the littlest announcement.

In those days, the early days of Pink, I was doing a lot of freelance editing for local small presses, which is to say that I spent many waking hours at my desk. Pink assessed my habits early on, and decided to make them her own; or perhaps she decided that she too was an editor. In any case she would come up to my lap, where she would sit, often looking up with something to say. She was in fact the only cat I have ever known with whom a sort of conversation was possible; we made sounds back and forth at each other, very politely, and though mine were mostly nonsense syllables, Pink seemed pleased.

Pink was her main name, about which Zoe Pinkerton was very happy. "Lordy, no one's ever named a cat for me before." But Andrew and I used many other names for her. I had an idea that Pink liked a new name occasionally; maybe we all would? In any case we called her a lot of other, mostly P-starting names: Peppercorn, Pipsy Doodler, Poipu Beach. This last was a favorite place of Zoe's, when she went out to "the islands." Pink seemed to like all those names; she regarded us both with her great gray eyes—especially me; she was always mostly my cat.

Worried about raccoons and Berkeley free-roaming dogs, we decided early on that Pink was to be a house cat, for good. She was not expendable. But Andrew and I liked to take weekend trips, and after she came to live with us we often took Pink along. She liked car travel right away; settled on the seat between us, she would join right in whenever we broke what had been a silence—not interrupting, just adding her own small voice, a sort of soft clear mew.

This must have been in the early seventies; we talked a lot about Nixon and Watergate. "Mew if you think he's guilty," Andrew would say to Pink, who always responded satisfactorily.

Sometimes, especially on summer trips, we would take Pink out for a semiwalk; our following Pink is what it usually amounted to, as she bounded into some meadow grass, with miniature leaps. Once, before I could stop her, she suddenly raced ahead—to a chipmunk. I was horrified. But then she raced back to me with the chipmunk in her mouth, and after a tiny shake she let him go, and the chipmunk ran off, unscathed. (Pink had what hunters call a soft mouth. Of course she did.)

We went to Rome and I missed her, very much; and we went off to the Piazza Argentina and gave a lot of lire to the very old woman there who was feeding all those mangy, half-blind cats. In honor of Pink.

I hope that I am not describing some idealized "perfect" adorable cat, because Pink was never that. She was entirely herself, sometimes cross and always independent. On the few occasions when I swatted her (very gently), she would hit me right back, a return swat on the hand—though always with sheathed claws.

I like to think that her long life with us, and then just with me, was a very happy one. Her version, though, would undoubtedly state that she was perfectly happy until Black and Brown moved in.

Another Berkeley lunch. A weekday, and all the women present work, and have very little time, and so this getting together seems a rare treat. Our hostess, a diminutive and brilliant art historian, announces that her cat, Parsley, is extremely pregnant. "Honestly, any minute," she laughs, and this is clearly true; the poor burdened cat, a brown Burmese, comes into the room, heavy and uncomfortable and restless. Searching.

A little later, in the midst of serving our many-salad lunch, the hostess says that the cat is actually having her kittens now, in the kitchen closet. We all troop out into the kitchen to watch.

The first tiny sac-enclosed kitten to barrel out is a black one, instantly vigorous, eager to stand up and get on with her life. Then three more come at intervals; it is harder to make out their colors.

"More multiple insemination," I told Andrew that night.

"It must be rife in Berkeley, like everyone says."

"It was fascinating, watching them being born."

"I guess, if you like obstetrics."

A month or so later the art historian friend called with a very sad story; she had just been diagnosed as being very clearly allergic to cats. "I thought I wasn't feeling too well, but I never thought it could be the cats. I know you already have that marvelous Pink, but do you think—until I find someone to take them? Just the two that are left?"

Surprisingly, Andrew, when consulted, said, "Well, why not? Be entertainment for old Pink; she must be getting pretty bored with just us."

We did not consult Pink, who hated those cats on sight. But Andrew was right away crazy about them, especially the black one (maybe he had wanted a cat of his own?). We called them, of course, Black and Brown. They were two Burmese females, or semi-Burmese, soon established in our house and seeming to believe that they lived there.

Black was (she is) the more interesting and aggressive of the two. And from the first she truly took to Pink, exhibiting the sort of clear affection that admits of no rebuff.

We had had Pink spayed as soon as she was old enough, after one quite miserable heat. And now Black and Brown seemed to come into heat consecutively, and to look to Pink for relief. She raged and scratched at them as they, alternatively, squirmed and rubbed toward her. Especially Brown, who gave all the signs of a major passion for Pink. Furious, Pink seemed to be saying, Even if I were the tomcat that you long for, I would never look at you.

Black and Brown were spayed, and relations among the cats settled down to a much less luridly sexual pattern. Black and Brown both liked Pink and wished to be close to her, which she would almost never permit. She refused to eat with them, haughtily waiting at mealtimes until they were through.

It is easy for me to imagine Black and Brown as people, as women. Black would be a sculptor, I think, very strong, moving freely and widely through the world. Unmarried, no children. Whereas Brown would be a very sweet and pretty, rather silly woman, adored by her husband and sons.

But I do not imagine Pink as a person at all. I only see her as herself. A cat.

Zoe was going to move to Hawaii, she suddenly said. "Somewhere on Kauai, natch, and probably Poipu, if those grubby developers have kept their hands off anything there." Her hatchet laugh. "But I like the idea of living on the islands, away from it all. And so does Gordon. You guys will have to come and visit us there. Bring Pink, but not those other two strays."

"Gordon" was a new beau, just turned up from somewhere in Zoe's complex Dallas childhood. With misgivings, but I think mostly goodwill, we went over to meet him, to hear about all these new plans.

Gordon was dark and pale and puffy, great black blotches

under his narrow, dishonest eyes, a practiced laugh. Meeting him, I right off thought, They're not going to Hawaii; they're not going anywhere together.

Gordon did not drink at all that day, although I later heard that he was a famous drunk. But occasionally he chided Zoe, who as usual was belting down vodka on ice. "Now Baby," he kept saying. (Strident, striding Zoe—Baby?) "Let's go easy on the sauce. Remember what we promised?" (We?)

At which Zoe laughed long and loud, as though her drinking were a good joke that we all shared.

A week or so after that Zoe called and said she was just out of the hospital. "I'm not in the greatest shape in the world," she said—and after that there was no more mention of Gordon, nor of a move to Hawaii.

And not very long after that Zoe moved down to Santa Barbara. She had friends there, she said.

Pink by now was in some cat equivalent to middle age. Still quite small, still playful at times, she was almost always talkative. She disliked Black and Brown, but sometimes I would find her nestled against one of them, usually Black, in sleep. I had a clear sense that I was not supposed to know about this occasional rapport, or whatever. Pink still came up to my lap as I worked, and she slept on our bed at night, which we had always forbidden Black and Brown to do.

We bought a new, somewhat larger house, farther up in the hills. It had stairs, and the cats ran happily up and down, and they seemed to thrive, like elderly people who benefit from a new program of exercise.

———

Andrew got sick, a terrible swift-moving cancer that killed him within a year, and for a long time I did very little but grieve. I sometimes saw friends, and I tried to work. There was a lot to do about Andrew's bookstore, which I sold, but mostly I stayed at home with my cats, all of whom were now allowed to sleep with me on that suddenly too-wide bed.

Pink at that time chose to get under the covers with me. In a peremptory way she would tap at my cheek or my forehead, demanding to be taken in. This would happen several times in the course of the night, which was not a great help to my already fragile pattern of sleep, but it never occurred to me to deny her. And I was always too embarrassed to mention this to my doctor when I complained of lack of sleep.

And then after several years I met Slater, at a well-meaning friend's house. Although as I have said I did not much like him at first, I was struck by his nice dark-red hair, and by his extreme directness—Andrew had a tendency to be vague; it was sometimes hard to get at just what he meant. Not so with Slater, who was very clear—immediately clear about the fact that he liked me a lot, and wanted us to spend time together. And so we became somewhat involved, Slater and I, despite certain temperamental obstacles, including the fact that he does not much like cats.

And eventually we began to plan a trip to Hawaii, where Slater had business to see to.

Pink as an old cat slept more and more, and her high-assed strut showed sometimes a slight arthritic creak. Her voice got appreciably louder; no longer a littlest announcer, her statements were loud and clear (I have to admit, it was not the most attractive sound). It seems possible that she was getting a little deaf. When

I took her to the vet, a sympathetic, tall, and handsome young Japanese woman, she always said, "She sure doesn't look her age—" at which both Pink and I preened.

The vet, Dr. Ino, greatly admired the stripes below Pink's neck, on her breast, which looked like intricate necklaces. I admired them too (and so had Andrew).

Needless to say, the cats were perfectly trained to the sand-box, and very dainty in their habits. But at a certain point I began to notice small accidents around the house, from time to time. Especially when I had been away for a day or two. It seemed a punishment, cat turds in some dark corner. But it was hard to fix responsibility, and I decided to blame all three—and to take various measures like the installation of an upstairs sand-box, which helped. I did think Pink was getting a little old for all those stairs.

Since she was an old cat I sometimes, though rarely, thought of the fact that Pink would die. Of course she would, eventually—although at times (bad times: the weeks and months around Andrew's illness and death) I melodramatically announced (more or less to myself) that Pink's death would be the one thing I could not bear. "Pink has promised to outlive me," I told several friends, and almost believed.

At times I even felt that we were the same person-cat, that we somehow inhabited each other. In a way I still do feel that— if I did not, her loss would be truly unbearable.

I worried about her when I went away on trips. I would always come home, come into my house, with some little appre-hension that she might not be there. She was usually the last of the three cats to appear in the kitchen, where I stood confused among baggage, mail, and phone messages. I would greet Black and Brown, and then begin to call her—"Pink, Pink?"—until, very diffident and proud, she would stroll unhurriedly toward me, and I would sweep her up into my arms with foolish cries of relief, and of love. *Ah, my darling old Pink.*

As I have said, Slater did not particularly like cats; he had nothing against them, really, just a general indifference. He eventually developed a fondness for Brown, believing that she liked him too, but actually Brown is a whore among cats; she will purr and rub up against anyone who might feed her. Whereas Pink was always discriminating, in every way, and fussy. Slater complained that one of the cats deposited small turds on the bathmat in the room where he sometimes showered, and I am afraid that this was indeed old Pink, both angry and becoming incontinent.

One night at dinner at my house, when Slater and I, alone, were admiring my view of the bay and of romantic San Francisco, all those lights, we were also talking about our trip to Hawaii. Making plans. He had been there before and was enthusiastic.

Then the phone rang, and it was Lucy, daughter of Zoe, who told me that her mother had died the day before, in Santa Barbara. "Her doctor said it was amazing she'd lived so long. All those years of booze."

"I guess. But Lucy, it's so sad, I'm so sorry."

"I know." A pause. "I'd love to see you sometime. How's old Pink?"

"Oh, Pink's fine," I lied.

Coming back to the table, I explained as best I could about Zoe Pinkerton, how we got Pink. I played it all down, knowing his feelings about cats. But I thought he would like the multiple-insemination part, and he did—as had Andrew. (It is startling when two such dissimilar men, Andrew, the somewhat dreamy book person, and Slater, the practical man, get so turned on by the same dumb joke.)

"So strange that we're going to Poipu," I told Slater. "Zoe

always talked about Poipu." As I said this I knew it was not the sort of coincidence that Slater would find remarkable.

"I'm afraid it's changed a lot," he said, quite missing the point. "The early developers have probably knocked hell out of it. The greedy competition."

So much for mysterious ways.

Two days before we were to go to Hawaii, in the morning Pink seemed disoriented, unsure when she was in her sandbox, her feeding place. Also, she clearly had some bad intestinal disorder. She was very sick, but still in a way it seemed cruel to take her to the vet, whom I somehow knew could do nothing for her. However, at last I saw no alternative.

She (Dr. Ino, the admirable vet) found a large hard mass in Pink's stomach, almost certainly cancer. Inoperable. "I just can't reverse what's wrong with her," the doctor told me, with great sadness. And succinctness: I saw what she meant. I was so terribly torn, though: Should I bring Pink home for a few more days—whatever was left to her—although she was so miserable, so embarrassed at her own condition?

I chose not to do that (although I still wonder, I still am torn). And I still cannot think of those last moments of Pink. Whose death I chose.

I wept on and off for a couple of days. I called some close friends who would have wanted to know about Pink, I thought; they were all most supportively kind (most of my best friends love cats).

And then it was time to leave for Hawaii.

Sometimes, during those days of packing and then flying to Hawaii, I thought it odd that Pink was not more constantly on my mind, even odd that I did not weep more than I did. Now, though, looking back on that trip and its various aftermaths, I see that in fact I was thinking about Pink all that time, that she was totally in charge, as she always had been.

We stayed in a pretty condominium complex, two-story white buildings with porches and decks, and everywhere sweeping green lawns, and flowers. A low wall of rocks, a small coarsely sanded beach, and the vast and billowing sea.

Ours was a second-floor unit, with a nice wide balcony for sunset drinks, or daytime sunning. And, looking down from that balcony one night, our first, I saw the people in the building next door, out on the grass beside what must have been their kitchen, *feeding their cats.* They must have brought along these cats, two supple gray Siamese, and were giving them their supper. I chose not to mention this to Slater, I thought I could imagine his reaction, but in the days after that, every time we walked past that building I slowed my pace and looked carefully for the cats, and a couple of times I saw them. Such pretty cats, and very friendly, for Siamese. Imagine: traveling to Hawaii with your cats—though I was not at all sure that I would have wanted Black and Brown along, nice as they are, and pretty.

Another cat event (there were four in all) came as we drove from Lihue back to Poipu, going very slowly over those very sedate tree- and flower-lined streets, with their decorous, spare houses. Suddenly I felt—we felt—a sort of thump, and Slater, looking startled, slowed down even further and looked back.

"Lord God, that was a cat," he said.

"A cat?"

"She ran right out into the car. And then ran back."

"Are you sure? She's all right?"

"Absolutely. Got a good scare though." Slater chuckled.

But you might have killed a cat, I did not say. And for a moment I wondered if he actually had, and lied, saying the cat was okay. However, Slater would never lie to spare my feelings, I am quite sure of that.

The third cat happening took place as we drove down a winding, very steep mountain road (we had been up to see the mammoth gorges cut into the island, near its western edge). On either side of the road was thick green jungle growth—and suddenly, there among the vines and shrubs, I saw a small yellow cat staring out, her eyes lowered. Frightened. Eyes begging.

Slater saw her too, and even he observed, "Good Lord, people dumping off animals to starve. It's awful."

"You're sure she doesn't live out there? a wilderness cat?"

"I don't think so." Honest Slater.

We did not talk then or later about going back to rescue that cat—not until the next day, when he asked me what I would like to do and I said, "I'd like to go back for that cat." He assumed I was joking, and I guess I mostly was. There were too many obvious reasons not to save that particular cat, including the difficulty of finding her again. But I remembered her face; I can see it still, that expression of much-resented dependence. It was a way even Pink looked, very occasionally.

Wherever we drove, through small neat impoverished "native" settlements (blocks of houses that Slater and his cohorts planned to buy, and demolish, to replace with fancy condos), with their lavish flowers all restrained into tiny beds, I kept looking at the yards, and under the houses. I wanted to see a cat, or some cats (I wanted to see Pink again). Realizing what I was doing, I continued to do it, to strain for the sight of a cat.

The fourth and final cat event took place as we walked home from dinner one night, in the flower-scented, corny-romantic

Hawaiian darkness. To our left was the surging black sea and to our right large tamed white shrubbery, and a hotel swimming pool, glistening darkly under feeble yellow floodlights. And then quite suddenly, from nowhere, a small cat appeared in our path, shyly and uncertainly arching her back against a bush. A black cat with some yellow tortoise markings, a long thin curve of a tail.

"He looks just like your Pink, doesn't he?" Slater actually said this, and I suppose he believed it to be true.

"What—Pink? But her tail—Jesus, didn't you even see my cat?"

I'm afraid I went on in this vein, sporadically, for several days. But it did seem so incredible, not remembering Pink, my elegantly striped, my tailless wonder. (It is also true that I was purposefully using this lapse, as one will, in a poor connection.)

I dreaded going home with no Pink to call out to as I came in the door. And the actuality was nearly as bad as my imaginings of it: Black and Brown, lazy and affectionate, glad to see me. And no Pink, with her scolding *hauteur,* her long-delayed yielding to my blandishments.

I had no good pictures of Pink, and to explain this odd fact I have to admit that I am very bad about snapshots; I have never devised a really good way of storing and keeping them, and tend rather to enclose any interesting ones in letters to people who might like them, to whom they would have some meaning. And to shove the others into drawers, among old letters and other unclassifiable mementos.

I began then to scour my house for Pink pictures, looking everywhere. In an album (Andrew and I put together a couple of albums, early on) I found a great many pictures of Pink as a tiny, tall-eared, brand-new kitten, stalking across a padded window seat, hiding behind an oversized Boston fern—among all the other pictures from those days: Zoe Pinkerton, happy and smoking a long cigarette and almost drunk, wearing outrageous colors, on the deck of her house. And Andrew and I, young and very happy, silly, snapped by someone at a party. Andrew in his bookstore, horn-rimmed and quirky. Andrew uncharacteristically working in our garden. Andrew all over the place.

But no middle-year or recent pictures of Pink. I had in fact (I then remembered) sent the most recent shots of Pink to Zoe; it must have been just before she (Zoe) died, with a silly note about old survivors, something like that. It occurred to me to get in touch with Lucy, Zoe's daughter, to see if those pictures had turned up among Zoe's "effects," but knowing the chaos in which Zoe had always lived (and doubtless died) I decided that this would be tactless, unnecessary trouble. And I gave up looking for pictures.

Slater called yesterday to say that he is going back to Hawaii, a sudden trip. Business. I imagine that he is about to finish the ruination of all that was left of Zoe's islands. He certainly did not suggest that I come along, nor did he speak specifically of our getting together again, and I rather think that he, like me, has begun to wonder what we were doing together in the first place. It does seem to me that I was drawn to him for a very suspicious reason, his lack of resemblance to Andrew: Whyever should I seek out the opposite of a person I truly loved?

But I do look forward to some time alone now. I will think about Pink—I always feel her presence in my house, everywhere. Pink, stalking and severe, ears high. Pink, in my lap, raising her head with some small soft thing to say.

And maybe, since Black and Brown are getting fairly old now too, I will think about getting another new young cat. Maybe, with luck, a small gray partially Manx, with no tail at all, and beautiful necklaces.

PART TWO

PART TWO

The Drinking Club

Harsh, powerful sunlight strikes the far edge of the giant pink bed on which Karen Brownfield, a pianist, now lies alone, Karen, on a concert tour. It must be midmorning, or nearly. On the other hand, perhaps early afternoon? Karen seems to have removed her watch; no doubt she has thrown it somewhere, or maybe given it away to someone (she did that once in Paris; she clearly remembers the boy's fair pretty face). However, wherever she is now and whatever time it is, what day, she is not in Paris. Karen is sure of that much.

Would knowing any more, though, improve her head, which threatens to split open like a watermelon in the sun? If she knew where she was, for example, would she feel any better?

She does not really believe that any such knowledge would help her. If she rang room service, and they told her, This is the Palmer House, in Cincinnati (if there is a Palmer House in Cincinnati), why would that improve her day? She doesn't see it, although her husband, a psychiatrist, undoubtedly would. Julian, Karen's husband, is committed to what he calls emotional information.

If she phoned Julian could he possibly tell her what went on last night here in her room? Well, of course not.

If she had played a concert, though, she would remember; she always does. And so, did she cancel a concert? That seems likely; quite possibly she canceled at about this same time yesterday, perhaps from this room, this bedside pink princess telephone. Noon is Karen's usual canceling time, her cop-out hour.

Whatever it was she did last night, for which she must have canceled her concert, made the most incredible whirlwind mess of the room. Karen closes her eyes against the sight of it: wadded-up clothes (hers), and sheets, so many sheets! all also wadded up. And knocked-over lamps, two of them on the floor. Full ashtrays. Karen doesn't smoke; they smell awful. Reeking glasses, partly filled with undrunk booze. Lord God, did she throw a party? *Who?*

What she can least well face, Karen has learned from other such mornings, is the sight of her own face. *I can't face my face,* she once thought, on some other occasion, and it almost made her laugh. She is surely not laughing now, though. She is seriously concerned with the logistics of getting in and out of the bathroom with no smallest glimpse of herself in any mirror. She knows that even if you wrap yourself in a sheet you are apt to see, but she manages not to.

Once back from the bathroom, where she found her watch (stopped), and where she was able to braid her hair without looking at it—she is good at this—Karen decides that what she really needs is something to drink. Then she can begin with the guilt over whatever went on last night. But first she will telephone Julian, in California.

If another person should enter that room, for instance the elderly black waiter delivering the wine that Karen is about to order (this hotel, which is famous, is in Atlanta), he would see, in addition to the mess, a woman whose face is the color of white linen. A crazy-looking woman, with the whitest face and the biggest eyes, dark lake-blue, and the longest, thickest rope of red hair that he has ever seen.

It is actually only about nine-thirty in Atlanta. Karen has slept less than she thinks she has. Thus in California it is about six-thirty.

It is early for a phone call, especially since Julian is not alone in his bed, their bed, his and Karen's. He is there with his lover, Lila Lewisohn, also a psychiatrist. ("Julian's *girl*," would be Karen's phrase for what Lila is—*girl*, with ugly emphasis—if Karen actually knew what she now only strongly suspects.)

This is something that Julian and Lila have never done before, slept together at Julian's house. Usually there are children at home, as well as Karen, and until recently there was Lila's husband to whom she had to return, Garrett Lewisohn, a lawyer.

And tonight, after dinner in Sausalito, they had meant to go back to Lila's house, on the western, seaward slope of San Francisco. However, as they approached the Golden Gate, the yellow fog lights and heavy traffic, they learned from another motorist that there had been an accident on the bridge, and it would be closed for at least another half hour. Not long to wait; ordinarily they would have done just that: Lila and Julian are accustomed to postponements, to deferral of pleasure. Tonight, though, for whatever reasons, an unusual mood of urgency was upon them (the wine, and the fact that they hadn't been together for several weeks, Julian having been occupied with holding Karen together for her tour). In the restaurant their hands often met, eyes meeting too, laughing but complicitous, sexual.

And so, "I don't want to wait, do you?" Julian.

"No. But—"

Julian however had begun to turn the car about and to head too fast toward Mill Valley. Up the winding road to his very large, ultracontemporary house, all glass and steel, among giant redwoods, mammoth ferns.

Lila has been there before, of course. She and Julian, after all, are colleagues. And the two couples, Julian and Karen, Garrett and Lila, were for a time ostensibly friends.

As lovers, though, Lila and Julian have mostly gone to motels for love, always as far from the city as they have had time for: Half Moon Bay, Bodega Bay—they seem to seek the coast. More recently, since Garrett left (moving down to Atherton with his pregnant young girlfriend), they have enjoyed the privacy—the incredibly luxury, it seems to them—of Lila's small but pleasant house.

Tonight, though, Julian's house. Or Karen's house. Her room. Her bed.

Just before the phone rings and long before any sunlight penetrates the morning fog that envelops Julian's house, naked Lila's very long brown legs are entangled in sheets, her upper body pressed to Julian's bare bony back. They breathe in unison, deeply.

(This is a scene that Karen has often imagined. Her most frequent and blackest fantasies are of Lila and Julian, in sexual poses. She has also thought of Julian with female patients; she has imagined him with some sad woman on the worn brown leather sofa in his office, humping away—although this seems much less likely than Julian with Lila.)

The phone bell. A soft, sudden, and terrible sound.

Both Julian and Lila, trained doctors, are instantly awake. And both, in the second before Julian answers it, think, Karen. Or maybe a patient; they both hope it will be a patient.

"This is Dr. Brownfield. Well Karen, of course I'm here, but my dear it is rather early. Six-thirty. Well, I know it's later where you are. Tuesday, you must be in Atlanta." He laughs, then coughs. "How is Atlanta? The concert? Well Karen, I'm really sorry. No I didn't—No I don't. Karen, I'm sorry. No I didn't. No of course I don't blame you. No one will—of course you can't play when you're sick. Yes it is unpredictable. No Karen, I am not mad at you. Yes, I do. No, I don't think I should come to Atlanta, even if I could. No. No. If you need a doctor—No Karen, I am not mad. Yes. Right. Good. Good for you. Good-bye. Love."

Hanging up, he leans back against the headboard and looks at Lila.

She sees that he is utterly, totally exhausted.

"Karen has a bad cold," says Julian. "She says."

"Oh." As though Karen could see her, Lila begins to pull sheets up around herself, covering bare breasts.

"She had to cancel the concert. Of course."

"By the way, what's your name?" Karen, in Atlanta, is speaking to the man who has brought her the wine, a man who is large and old and black, with big gnarled hands. The bottle that he has brought on a napkined silver tray is tall and green, cold, glistening rivulets running down its sides.

"Calvin Montgomery, ma'am."

"Oh Lord, please don't call me ma'am. My name is Karen. Mrs. Brownfield. But you have a beautiful name."

"Thank you, Mrs. Brown. Field."

Karen laughs. "And now if you could just open it. I'm a pianist, but I feel all thumbs today. Plus which I've got a cold." She laughs again.

As she watches him closely, eagerly, Calvin Montgomery with his big hands uncorks the wine in a single practiced gesture. "There you are. There's your cold cure."

They both laugh.

"Oh, Mr. Montgomery, thank *you*."

"Shall I make breakfast here?" Julian asks this of Lila. They are now sitting up in bed, both with sheets drawn up around them.

Looking at Julian, his thinning gray-brown hair, large sad and gray eyes, Lila thinks as she has before of the deep affinities binding them to each other. We could be brother and sister, she has sometimes thought. Blood ties.

"I don't think breakfast," she tells him. "I don't feel quite, you know, easy here." Knowing that he must feel the same about her being there. "I'd rather my house. If we have to eat breakfast."

"Well, something? Orange juice?" Julian has gotten up, is pulling on a robe. "You'll feel better after some juice," he reminds her.

Lila smiles, grateful. "Or I could just go home. But my car." Her car of course has been left in San Francisco, and suddenly this transportation problem seems both insuperable and highly symbolic. They are surely not supposed to sleep in this house.

Tendrils of fog reach around the smallest branches of Julian's huge redwoods, mysterious white feathers. And from somewhere comes the gentle, ambiguous sound of mourning doves, their softly descending notes.

I am simply not used to being here, Lila thinks, standing up and beginning to get into her clothes. I've never seen it before in the daytime, or almost day. All this fog. Julian is right, she thinks, I need some juice. Blood sugar.

The wine makes Karen feel at the same time physically improved and considerably worse in her head. As shadows disperse and she begins to remember.

An interview. Yesterday about this time, or was it later? At lunch? Yes, lunch. In any case, she was being interviewed in a strange restaurant in the below-street-level part of this hotel. A more famous, possibly preferable restaurant is billed as "rooftop," to Karen a terrifying word. And so, this subterranean room, all stones and small calculated waterfalls, and walls of sheet water, quite effective really but slightly scaring.

Her interviewer is a pale and puffy young man, with a small rosy mouth and blinking white-blue eyes. A Southern, very Southern voice.

At first he was hard to understand, but gradually, after the skirmishes of small talk, he began to come through. "Married to a psychiatrist," he was saying. "Must be extremely interesting. Though I don't suppose they talk a lot about their cases, not supposed to anyways. But don't you find it just the least little bit of what you might call a threat?"

"Oh, I do," Karen said. No one, certainly not the shrink that she herself once went to, though not for long, has ever quite asked this. And Karen realized that from the start she had felt something very sympathetic about this young man. Karen likes fat people; she finds them comforting. Julian is so extremely thin, all sharp bones and stretched dry skin.

"I don't need to tell you that the question is solely motivated by a personal curiosity," the young man assured her, blinking, signaling his commitment to truth. Hal, did he say his name was? Yes. Hal.

"I've just put in so much time with those fellows and lady shrinks too, that for the life of me I can't imagine a home life with any one of them," said Hal.

"Oh, you're absolutely right," Karen told him. And then she confided, "I think I'm coming down with a really bad cold. Can you hear it in my voice?"

"Oh, I sure can. Well, maybe this here ice tea was a mistake." At first this seemed an odd remark, and then not odd. Karen recognized a certain gleam in those pale eyes, along with a certain timid question in his voice.

"I'm sure you're right," she told him, laughing lightly and tossing her long braid back over her shoulder. "We need some stronger stuff. What do folks around here mostly drink?" (Lord, where had she suddenly got that accent?)

"Bourbon, mostly. Although I've gone off that hard stuff myself." Righteous Hal. "But I can tell you, there's a certain very nice concoction—" He snapped his fingers for the waiter.

The concoction when it came was fairly sweet and very strong. Karen could tell it was strong. And watching Hal as he drank, his eager quick repeated sips, she thought, No wonder I like you.

They had a couple of concoctions, all the time talking in a very civilized way about Karen's professional history, Hal taking notes: Wellesley, Juilliard, the Paris Conservatory. Brahms, Chopin, Debussy.

And then, maybe on the third of those drinks, they returned to the question of shrinks. Living with them. Talking to them. The terror.

"Most probably in their spare time they ought to just only talk to each other," Hal said (fatally).

"Oh, you are so right," Karen told him. "My husband, Julian Brownfield, has this big friend, and when I say big I mean really, really big, you never in your life saw such a big tall woman. Name of Lila Lewisohn." And out it all poured, in that crazy new sweet Southern voice. All Karen's worst fears, her ugliest, most powerful fantasies.

"I can just see her big long legs in some great big old bed, some motel I guess, all wrapped around my skinny white old Julian."

Along with the new accent Karen seemed to have acquired a new persona, and one that she liked a lot. She liked being a silly, pretty, somewhat flirty, complaining little woman, talking to that nice big fat old boy. Telling him just about everything.

Her cold by then was making her sniffle and sneeze, and quite naturally Karen had a lot to say about her condition. "It's still just coming on strong. I can feel it all over me," she told Hal. "Although these concoctions of yours are really something else. But you know if you'll just excuse me I think I've got to call my agent. There's just no way I can play a concert tonight. As a matter of fact I think I'd better make the call from my room. Why don't you just come on up with me, give me some moral support? Lord God, will he be *mad*! I'm telling you, fit to kill."

So far Karen remembers it all, the whole conversation now plays as precisely as a tape, in her grimed, exhausted mind.

Now, continuing in her new Southern voice, she thinks, Julian wasn't very nice to me on the phone. He tells me he cares how I feel, but he doesn't, not really. All he really cares about is his patients, and that awful old Lila.

Julian and Lila have left Mill Valley, crossed the bridge, and reached San Francisco, Lila's house. But although alone in those familiar surroundings they are not quite restored to each other. For one thing there is almost no time. Both have morning patients; Julian must leave. And for another Karen is so present to them both, having just arisen from her bed, been awakened by her voice.

Lila has made coffee and heated two bagels. With this small nourishment they are perched at Lila's round kitchen table. It would be pleasant simply to enjoy the moment for what it is, but the fact of what they are, what they do, prevents an avoidance of the subject. Of Karen.

Julian. "Amazing, really amazing. I still feel a certain amount of guilt over not going to Atlanta."

Lila. "Julian the caretaker."

"I know; we seem to have struck a perfect balance, she and I."

"Right. Whereas Garrett and I were so unbalanced that he had to leave. Or one of us did and it turned out to be him." But they have already talked a great deal about Garrett—of course they have. They have even discussed at some length the possibility of their needing Garrett for some balance of their own: Since Julian is married to Karen, how will things work out in terms of Julian and Lila, now that Lila is unmarried? They talk a lot, they speculate.

Not so long ago, all four of those people sat at that same round kitchen table, Lila and Garrett playing host to Julian and Karen. All drinking champagne, good French stuff bought by Garrett. And they were eating something fancy that he had whipped up, crab and mushrooms. After a concert of Karen's, in Berkeley.

Karen had played beautifully. Brahms, Mozart, Debussy. A silly Satie. A safe concert, as reviewers would hasten to point out (Karen was unpopular with local critics; her habit of cancellation did not win friends), but still, Karen's particular lyric flow was present. Playing, she sang. Wonderfully.

That night Lila, as she looked at Karen, the small exhausted woman hunched over the table, her fallen silk hair a mess, white hands gripping the stem of her glass (Karen tended to break glasses; she did so later, a good glass from Lila's mother; Garrett was angry)—watching Karen, then, it seemed astounding to Lila that she could have played at all.

Karen's beauty, too, was always astounding, even totally disheveled, entirely tired. That white, translucent skin, the very wide, dark-blue eyes, small nose, and long delicate mouth. The amazing long red silk hair.

Sometimes, envisioning Karen, Lila has thought, Well, no wonder. No wonder Julian wants her around just to look at, even if she is so often drunk, impossible. She is so beautiful, and impressively talented. He feels what I would feel, probably.

"I have this really wonderful group of friends at home," Karen now remembers telling Hal, once they were up in her room and she had made the phone call. "All people who like to drink, well, you know, too much. And who've tried the shrink route, A.A., Betty Ford, all that grim stuff. Well, we all got together and we formed this little club, we called it the Drinking Club. We meet every now and then and we really drink, I mean we just drink up a storm. But the rest of the time, stone-cold sober."

By the time she had finished all this about her club, both Karen and Hal were laughing so hard they were crying, she sitting up on her big pink bed and he in a chair near the window— a huge piece of floor-to-ceiling glass that seemed to slant into the room.

"Only trouble was," Karen continued, "we got to having our meetings all the *time*."

"You know what?" Hal said, when either of them could

speak. "You know what, I'm going to start me a branch of your club right here in Atlanta, and I'm going to start promoting the first meeting right here in this room, right *now*."

And Hal picked up the bedside pink princess phone and began to tap out numbers, and to talk. In the mirror across the room Karen could see herself as he did so: a pretty little woman lying back on the bed, her loosened hair fanned out, prettily (the same bed which is now such a horrible mess).

Yesterday afternoon? Last night? As Hal talked and talked on the phone Karen lay back and laughed and laughed, his voice sounded so funny to her, just killing. And his fat was so nice, so reassuring.

After that her memory is vague, more spotty.

Other people came to her room. All men? Karen thinks so, but just as she thinks, All men, she remembers a woman. Was that a maid, with more drinks, bottles? Ice?

Drinking. Smoking. A lot of them smoked, a lot.

Then something about the air conditioner not working. Too hot.

People undressing?

But no sex. Nothing like that.

Or was there?

At that moment, two things happen to Karen simultaneously. Her memory closes down. Black. Blank. And her stomach lurches, then tightens like a fist.

In the bathroom nothing comes to her mouth but bile, thin and bitter, greenish. Her stomach contracts again, and again. More bitterness, more thin bile.

Very clearly then, to herself Karen says, This must never happen again. Not any of it. Not ever.

She begins to repeat, "I am an alcoholic. I am not in control of my life."

In San Francisco, in the heavy early-morning fog that will probably last all day, the trees around Lila's house drip moisture, water running down pine needles, slow drops from eucalyptus leaves. And from out in the bay comes the heavy, scraping sound of foghorns.

Lila has pulled a dark gray sweater over the silk shirt that she wore to dinner last night, with Julian, but even so she is cold as they stand there in her doorway, saying good-bye.

"Well, in any case, tonight, okay?" asks Julian. "We'll stay here? Do you want to make dinner, or should we go out, do you think? It might be better—"

This tentativeness of Julian's tells Lila that he is not at all sure what to do about Karen, who might telephone—anywhere.

Surprising herself—she, too, had assumed this night for them together—Lila hears her own voice saying, "Well, maybe not? I mean maybe not tonight at all?" She laughs to lighten the effect of what she has said: they have never before not seen each other when they could. "Let's talk on the phone instead." She laughs again.

"Well. Oh. Well, okay." Looking hard at Lila as he says those few words, Julian too seems to strive for lightness. But then he says, "Or I could make dinner at my house? We haven't done that for a while. I'll bring you home early, I promise."

Meaning that he can't quite let her go, not now? He needs some sort of help from Lila?

No time for talking about it, however, and so she temporizes. "Well, let me call you later, okay?"

They kiss, both with the thought that they will see each other that night after all. Probably.

Julian walks over to his car, and Lila goes back inside her house, where she will clean up their few dishes before heading over to her study, ready for the day's first patient.

————

Cleaning up her room, which seemed to Karen a first step, is not quite as terrible as she imagined it would be. To start with, there are not as many sheets lying around as she thought there were. She pulls the sheets and a couple of towels into a bundle that she then thrusts out into the hall—seeing no one in the corridor, luckily.

She empties the ashtrays into the toilet, along with the inches of booze in the several glasses. Flushes it all away. Gone. She considers washing the ashtrays and decides against it, imagining that wet-ash smell. She just stacks everything there in the bathroom and closes the door.

Well. Already a huge improvement.

She will call her agent and apologize; in fact she will call a lot of people, explaining, apologizing. But there is no way, not now, that she could go on to New York today, as she was meant to do.

She will call down for some food, a tray of tea and eggs, some yogurt, all healthy stuff. Maybe that nice black man will bring it up to her, the one who brought the wine. (Wine. She will never drink wine again, or anything else.) How surprised and pleased he will be to see how she has tidied up the room! And to see her looking so much better! How surprised everyone will be when they see her.

She very much hopes it will be the same waiter. She really liked him. If only she could remember his name.

Patients

The young woman in the chair across from Lila's (Dr. Lewi-sohn's) chair, the new patient, who is shredding Kleenex into her smart black leather lap—that young woman in some general, overall way is lying. All Lila's instincts inform her that what she is hearing now from this young woman is false. Not the specifics: the busy, older husband impatient with the new baby and still wanting to have a lot of dinner parties; the baby herself with colic; and this sad, pretty red-haired girl trying hard to balance it all, in a too-large, too-fancy new house. All that is undoubt-edly true, but at the same time some large-scale lie is there. What is wrong with this big picture?

Lila regards her patient, and she sees:

Short, very curly red hair and pale friendly freckles across a small nose. Small stubby nervous hands. Perhaps she is an alco-holic? This could be the significant, hidden fact. It is possible, but Lila now identifies a false association of her own: Karen Brownfield, the red-haired wife of Julian Brownfield, who is Lila's lover and also a psychiatrist, is an alcoholic. Apart from the red hair this woman, this "Jane Bates," does not look at all like Karen, who is beautiful, not pretty, pale and unfreckled.

"Uh, John," says Jane Bates. "When we were going together

he was so great. Exciting. Uh, incredible in some way. You know, uh, sex. But now—" All that was said rather hesitantly, and now Jane bursts out, "Oh Jesus, it's all so trite, you know? I can't stand it. The big romance that goes stale once you're married. Everyone knows that story. Why do women keep getting married? Are all of us crazy, do you think?"

"Surely no crazier than men are." Lila smiles. "But that does seem a fairly familiar pattern." Precisely her own pattern, she is thinking: her very rash first, young marriage, and more recently, less forgivably, her supposedly mature, considered marriage to Garrett, a lawyer—an incredible illicit lover, a bored and boring husband, who recently left Lila for a younger woman. An even more trite story.

But what is the major lie that Lila is being told by this new patient, Jane Bates? Is she possibly a rock star, someone famous in a world that Lila might well not know? This seems unlikely; nothing in this sad, mild young woman's demeanor suggests fame, or success. However, Lila now feels that she has picked up some as yet unconscious clue to her own certain sense of distrust. Could it have to do with the patient's blank, too-ordinary name?

"This room is so nice and small," says the patient. "It's where you live?"

"No, this is my office. My study. I live in the small house where you parked."

"Oh of course. You live alone?" is the next question, then covered over with a hurried, "I guess you don't tell patients much about yourself."

Neutrally: "No, I don't. But do you want to tell me more about your house?"

Six bedrooms. An acre of gardens, or maybe two acres? Jesus, Jane doesn't even know. Supposedly two gardeners, and a housekeeper and a baby nurse, and a janitorial service. So much, just keeping track of all those people. Plus baby doctors. Caterers for parties. And the husband, John.

All this is in Atherton where, a minor coincidence, Lila herself grew up, in a somewhat similar though even grander older house—it now seems a hundred years ago. Lila's house has recently been sold (at last, thank God) and so she knows about Atherton real-estate values.

The weather outside the long windows of Lila's office is menacing, dark gray and cold. Heavily fogged. August in California, Lila's most hated month. But for whatever private idiosyncratic reasons she resists taking off the month that most psychiatrists choose to take. ("You stick around to suffer," Garrett sometimes accused her.) In any case her mind now wanders—with more than one variety of envy—to Julian Brownfield, her lover, who is now in Maine, with beautiful Karen, formerly a concert pianist, now drying out from her many years of booze.

But, Maine. As Jane the patient goes on and on about her baby's colic, her husband's inability to hear her, Lila remembers Maine: clean white silky beaches and small dark intimate islands, far out in the water. Clear bright days in August, and cool clear starred nights. The Northern Lights. Shooting stars.

She is jolted from such thoughts, though, by a single word, a name, clearly spoken in error. *Garrett.* Her new patient, "Jane Bates," though speaking of her own husband, "John," referred to him as Garrett.

So, Lila's mind whirls. This is not Jane Bates, of course not. This young woman is Phyllis, new wife of Garrett. New wife, new baby, Atherton house. Of course.

Furious, even angrier than such an imposture has given her every right to be, Lila breathes deeply, willing control. She is aware that she is staring, clutching her chair—and wills herself to stop. "You're Phyllis," she finally (unnecessarily) says.

Phyllis, referred to by Garrett as Phylly (once Lila had smiled at the silly pun: the silly Phylly)—Phyllis now brings the useless Kleenex up to her eyes. She has begun again to cry. "This was all my idea, not Garrett's," is the first thing she is able to say.

"I'm sure." Dry-eyed, still-angry Lila. "But you know of course that it is out of the question for me to see you as a patient."

"I knew that, I just—" More sobs take over.

There is nothing for Lila to do but sit this out, as it were, she feels. At the end of this hour another patient will come to save her from poor weeping Phyllis. And in a coolly objective way, Lila now congratulates her own unconscious for having recognized this deception, really from the start.

"I just had to see you," Phyllis tells her, when she can speak. "Garrett talks about you. Comparisons. Your dinners. I guess I thought in a way he'd be sort of pleased. I mean if I'd got away with it. A joke on you."

Lila is aware of a half smile on her own face. "Well, I guess it didn't quite work out."

"No. But I do need a shrink. Very much. Obviously." More tears.

Lila hesitates. "I don't think I should be the person to recommend one. But the Psychoanalytic Society—" Her voice has become brisk, depersonalized.

Surprisingly, as Lila is speaking, Phyllis abruptly gets to her feet, so that Lila notes how small she is (well, of course Garrett would choose to follow an over-six-foot wife with one barely five feet tall). Phyllis is small and determined, probably bossy at times. And Lila sees that her resemblance to Karen Brownfield was not only red hair: Karen too is a small and willfully determined person.

No longer weeping, Phyllis says again, "I'm sorry. Just think of it as a bad joke. Okay?"

Lila smiles. "I'll try to. In any case, good luck."

"Thanks, Lila."

Karen and Julian Brownfield's hotel on the coast of Maine is new: pale blond-paneled rooms with accents of blue: blue painted fish, blue flowers here and there. The long wide windows look out to the grassy dunes, and to the sea, now a dark azure, with white-capped waves. Two small dark-wooded islands are juxtaposed, out there in the Atlantic.

More immediately in the foreground are a smooth new lawn, very green, and a modest circular blue swimming pool, now populated by two young families, with children. On the lawn another young father is running back and forth with a kite that will not rise—probably he is doing something wrong. His small daughter runs just behind him, laughing in the sun, not at all worried about the kite. So far whatever her father does is wonderful.

Julian and Karen have remained in their rooms, their two-story "suite" from which Julian at the window now worries about the kite, and that father. Sad Julian, who has just said to Karen, "You know you'd feel better if you could swim a little." He was unable not to say this, as earlier he could not help advising breakfast, and a walk—all declined, as he knew they would be.

Looking at Karen, Julian thinks it is the round curve of her forehead that most nearly breaks his heart. She has got so thin, with no booze and rather little food, that all her bones are apparent, and especially that child-shaped skull, with its curves and deep wide eye sockets. Her delicately indented chin is sharper now, and her cheekbones protuberant. Possibly she has never seemed so beautiful.

The clinician in Julian reminds him that when Karen's looks

at long last go, when no one falls in love with her for months, and then years, she may indeed be in serious trouble. A major depression, massive. So far, though, no loss of looks has even begun. Through the ravages of love affairs (two that Julian knows about, has picked up the pieces after, so to speak), through God knows how many drinks—through all that Karen has remained very, very beautiful. Vicissitudes, it would seem, have only added variety to her beauty. Indeed, Julian has been presented by his wife with a spectrum of lovely, red-haired women, from plumply voluptuous to just-not-gaunt, from warm and radiant smiles to the most poignant melancholy. Julian has had a succession of love affairs and marriages with all these women, all of whom are Karen.

Which is one of the reasons why they are still together, Julian believes. Another reason being the fact that he himself is the perfect, paradigmatic co-alcoholic.

He is also the perfect example of what people mean when they say that all shrinks are nuts. Julian knows this, and it affords him a certain bleak amusement: a successful (in his work, very successful) psychiatrist, who remains married to a beautiful, promiscuous alcoholic. Pretty funny, all around. It is quite true, psychiatrists are more truly mad than their patients are.

At the moment Karen is deeply engaged in doing her nails, in painting each long oval a glossy wild bright pink. One of the wonderful perks, as Karen has put it, about her "retirement" (she has given up the piano altogether; no concerts certainly and now no practicing either) is that now she can have marvelous long nails. And her nails would seem to have responded to this wish: they are indeed extremely long, and they look to be steel hard.

If Karen were as depressed now as in some ways she presents herself as being, would she be doing her nails? Would she care, still, for such a surface of perfection? Well, actually she might.

As though to answer him Karen holds up her hands and laughs. "See? Wild Pink. It's wonderful not even to have to look like a pianist. Who'd guess? Now my toes." And she starts to remove her sandals, to inspect her feet.

"I wonder why really we came to Maine." Julian had not meant to say this, and he prevents himself from adding: If you don't want to swim or even go for walks. He does say, "I don't think you much like it here."

"I don't like the inside of my head, that's the problem. As you know."

"Well yes, I do know."

Karen's toenails, which she has begun to wipe clean with a washcloth, then dry tenderly with a linen towel—all that will immobilize her for almost another hour, Julian knows. Which suddenly fills him with the most impossible impatience. He asks her, "You don't mind if I go for a walk?"

"Darling, of course not." This has come out deep-Southern, an accent that Karen for reasons of her own affects occasionally. Since her one visit down there: a canceled concert, in Atlanta.

"Sometimes I think you only like it in New York, or Boston." Again, Julian has spoken without quite meaning to. Without weighing words, that is.

Karen giggles, a nondepressed sound. "Well, indeed I do. I just might decide to live in one of those cities. Sometimes."

Julian walks along the beach, squeaking the fine white sand with his California running shoes. Tall and bent, walking slowly, he is considering yet again his wife of almost twenty-five years. And two things occur to him: one, Karen is not as depressed as she sometimes has been (and will be again, if his prediction for her old age holds true). And, two, it is possible, at least possible, that he, Julian, the husband-lover-custodian—that he is not doing her any good, in any role.

None of these thoughts is exactly new. God knows they are not, but Julian knows that he has resisted the latter perception, that of his own uselessness, partly out of what could be labeled misplaced professional pride.

Also, in the bright, very clean Maine air every thought has greater clarity. His whole mind seems to have been exposed to new light.

Concentrating mostly on the sand, along with his meditations, Julian now looks up to see a phone booth incongruously lodged against some sand dunes, sharply tilted but with a look of functioning.

His watch informs him that it is ten-twenty. In San Francisco three hours earlier. He could just catch Lila at breakfast, before her first patient.

He was right. The phone works.

"What a lovely surprise," Lila tells him, her voice warm, a little hoarse, and infinitely familiar. And startled: she would not have expected to hear from him at all.

Julian laughs, mostly from the sheer pleasure of being in contact with her. "Funniest thing," he tells her. "I was walking along the beach with my heavy thoughts and there before me was a functioning phone booth. Like a signal."

"Oh. Well, how good." Lila pauses, then asks, "Well, how's Maine?"

"Maine is beautiful. So clean. Even the water tastes terrific." He adds, "Karen hates it, I think. I wonder if I brought her here for some kind of punishment."

"I doubt that." Supportive Lila.

He asks, "What's going on with you?"

She seems to hesitate, then laughs a little. "An odd thing, actually. Garrett's new wife, the Phylly, came to see me more or less disguised as a patient."

"Well. What're you going to do about it?"

"I'm going to have a talk with Garrett. I guess I'll have to. She's in bad shape.

"Darling Julian, I have to go. How wonderful that you called."

"Lila, I love you. Seriously."

She laughs. "Me too. *Seriously.*"

And Julian emerges from the leaning phone booth, out into the pure bright sunshine, the slowly warming day.

A week or so later, having just come in from her studio after a very long day of patients, Lila sighs, and shivers. Her small house feels chilled, slightly damp, as though the blanketing fog that all day has lain so heavily over the city had penetrated her house, seeping through window cracks and under doors. She can almost imagine her house to be filled with fog.

Going over to light the fire, she is aware of an unpleasant anticipation, of not looking forward to the next hour or so. Garrett Lewisohn is coming by after work to have a "brief chat" (they both have used this phrase) about Phyllis. The Phylly.

Living here, Garrett always disliked this house. It was not at all a part of what he believed he had married, in Lila: a woman out of Atherton, a woman of substance. A woman far more like Lila's mother, actually—formidable, austere Henrietta—than like Lila herself. Henrietta had died before Garrett's entrance into Lila's life; still, he saw the house. It is almost too perfect that he should now have an Atherton house of his own—a house that is driving his young wife mad.

And it is perfect that Lila should be living alone in her own small, cozy, shabby house, with its drafts and creaks, and its magnificent surrounding grove of redwoods and eucalyptus. Its views of the bay and the bridge, the billowing green hills of Marin.

Lila has counted on the established fact of Garrett's punctuality, and thus by the appointed hour she is entirely ready, at least superficially: her hair combed, face powdered (a little). She has even changed her shoes, discarding the flat-heeled comfort necessary to hours of listening for some slightly smarter pumps. Waiting, she uneasily wanders—reflecting on the annoyance of waiting for someone you don't really want to see.

In the instant of entertaining that thought, however, there is Garrett, his car going just too fast in her drive. Brakes, a slam. Light racing footsteps, over gravel, then his knock.

On previous occasions, they have resolved the question of an appropriate gesture for a greeting; they shake hands. It was Garrett who instigated this, to Lila's considerable relief. Under these circumstances, the brushing, social kiss so promiscuously in vogue would seem even more false than it usually does.

Garrett, in his narrow dark suit, pale shirt, and heavy striped silk tie looks elegant and tired, harassed. As usual, in a hurry. But what he first says is, "Lila, you look great. Better than ever," which is not at all a usual remark for Garrett. "Not living with me would seem to agree with you," he adds, with a smile.

"Can I get you a drink?"

"Perrier?"

"Calistoga okay?"

All that dealt and dispensed with, they settle in Lila's living room, rather consciously not in their usual places (what was usual when they were together): Lila is on the edge of the leather sofa rather than in her habitual comfortable chair, and Garrett stands, having explained, "I've been sitting all day. Depositions."

"Actually me too." And looked up at Garrett, although she smiles, Lila thinks, How could we ever have married? how could I? As she has thought before.

"You do know," Garrett next tells her, "it was not my idea. Phyllis coming to see you."

"I really didn't think it was."

He frowns, looking out at the fog, fog that seems wind-propelled, pushing against the long windows.

"She is in bad shape though," says Garrett. "As you must have seen. She cries, she really cries a lot."

This has been said less by way of complaint, though, than in a sort of appalled sympathy, or so Lila hears it, and she is touched, Garrett not being a generally empathetic person. She tells him, "I think she's extremely tired, for one thing. Sometimes very tired people just cry."

"But we have, we have what I thought was a lot of help. Can you imagine the bills?" He pauses, perhaps feeling that that last was a mistake. "Well," he concedes, "maybe not enough help."

"Why don't you give her three months of no dinner parties?" Lila was unable not to say this, although she had earlier resolved against any specific suggestions—or any suggestions at all.

"But," says Garrett, with his small familiar frown, "but just now—" And then he subsides, allowing his seasonal objections to lapse (Lila knows that he is thinking of the coming fall, which is opera and large-party time, in San Francisco). "That's not a bad idea," he surprisingly grants.

Digesting this unusual docility, in Garrett, who likes a fight to the finish, generally, Lila concludes that he must be seriously concerned about Phyllis. For which she likes him better than she often does.

"Tell me something," Garrett asks next, with his thin-lipped, slightly sneering smile (except that now the sneer seems directed at himself, Lila feels). "Do you think I'm exceptionally selfish? Do I really never listen? I know you're a fair-minded woman."

Trying at first not to smile, Lila then does smile. Well, why not? But she feels that he deserves a serious answer. "You're pretty selfish," she tells him. "Of course most people are. And it's true, you're really not a very good listener."

"That's what I've been told." The sneer has become a scowl, intensely self-mocking.

He then asks her, "Do you think you might marry again?"

"Lord no." Lila laughs at her own vehemence. "I'm sure twice is enough. Probably some people shouldn't marry at all."

"I could be one of them." Garrett sighs deeply. "Sometimes I think men need marriage more than women do. Am I becoming a feminist?"

"I hope so." Lila laughs again. And then, knowing that she must, she says, "About Phyllis, though. Do you want me to give you some names? People she could see?"

Garrett stares at her, clearly not thinking about Phyllis. After a moment he says, "This may sound foolish, or impertinent, but what I would really like would be to take you to bed. Right now."

After a moment of another sort of staring on her own part, Lila flares out at him. "That would really help Phyllis a lot. Honestly, Garrett. Even if I—"

"Don't get mad. I'm harmless." Garrett attempts a smile.

"No you're not." Lila's face is heated, she hopes invisibly. She is indeed very angry.

"I'm sorry," he says. "It was just a thought. You do look great. You know you could be flattered."

"But I'm not." Standing up, Lila goes over to her desk, where she finds a pad of paper, a pen. Quickly she writes three names, and hands the list to Garrett.

It is obvious that she wishes him to go, and Lila does not choose to pretend otherwise. She simply says, "Well, I hope something helps."

"Christ, me too." He extends his hand to her. "Well, Lila. Thanks."

They shake hands, and Garrett is gone. Again.

Possibly because it is to be their last day in Maine, Karen, on that keenly bright Sunday morning seems considerably better (this is Julian's interpretation). She seems more alert, if not genuinely happy. On their way along the trim, newly graveled pathway to breakfast, in the main lodge, she exclaims at the smells. "It's so clean here," she says. "Smell the sea! I think I actually may go swimming later." And she smiles up at Julian, brilliantly, all pearl teeth and pale pink mouth, and warm blue eyes. "And what's that other smell?" she asks him. "It's so sharp and familiar. Nice. Oh, I know, it's tan bark, see? all around the flowers. Like children's playgrounds."

At breakfast, Karen decides that she won't after all go swimming, though. "But you go, Ju. You've hardly at all."

"Do you still feel like Portland for lunch?"

"Oh sure, that could be fun. In the meantime I'll be deciding what to wear." That last is their version of a family joke: Karen indeed spends a lot of time deciding what to wear.

And so, an hour or so later, Julian heads out over the slatted wooden walk that protects bare feet from the heavy, rough sea grasses. To the beach. And as though he would not have a lot of time he quickly drops his towel on the sand and starts to wade out, moving strongly in the cold, most beautifully clear green water. Beginning to swim, he is instantly exhilarated, feeling power, a muscular, cellular excitement. His whole long, strong body is involved in the pull, the stretch and forward thrust of his motion through the waves. His pleasure is almost sexual in its intensity, its totality. He imagines Lila's body all stretched in the act of swimming, or of love. In Mexico. Wherever.

He swims out in the direction of the small darkly wooded islands, which turn out to be considerably farther away than they looked to be from the shore. He would have liked to reach them, in a small way to explore; however, at the point that he judges to be about halfway there, he also decides that he has swum about half as far as he can (besides, there is the question of Karen, who is alone. Who has recently been depressed. There is always that: Karen alone). Treading water for a moment or two, reestablishing breath, Julian still looks toward those islands. "I almost swam out to some wonderful small islands," he will say to Lila. "The story of my life."

Back on the beach he towels himself—more pleasure, the rough sun-warmed toweling on his lively awakened skin.

Suicide: this has always been an issue, a fact of Julian's life, long before Karen and her perilous depressions. There was an uncle, and then a college friend. And an early patient, for whom Julian "did everything," for whom nothing helped, who escaped from Presbyterian Hospital to the Golden Gate Bridge. And with Karen it is simply there, her possible death in that way, a horrifying constant, of which he does not any longer so much think as feel.

It was of course much worse, say ten years back, when both Karen's drinking and her depressions began to get out of hand.

But he still feels, always, horribly, that he might come back to wherever Karen is, and find her dead. Or simply gone (that has happened a couple of times). He does not think of this in a conscious way anymore. Or, not often.

Nevertheless, he finds himself hurrying toward the wing of the hotel in which their rooms are. Up the flight of stairs to their suite, to the door. Unlocked.

Entering, he instantly knows that their rooms are empty, although still he calls out, *Karen,* several times, as he walks through the downstairs living room and small useless kitchen, the tiny bedroom in which he slept. He goes upstairs, hearing more silence, to the large room that was Karen's, that looks out to the sea grass and dunes, the beach and the sea, the small islands to which he almost swam. Had she looked out (unlikely somehow that she should have), Karen could have seen him there.

He looks at the unmade bed, the big floppy pillows, and sees a note, a large white sheet of paper, displayed there. (On other occasions Karen has chosen the unmarked exit, no explanatory notes in her wake. Lila: "Do you have any idea how incredibly inconsiderate, among other things, that is?")

This note is fairly long, for someone who dislikes and on the whole distrusts the written word.

Darling Ju, Roger called from Boston, must have just got my card. Anyway desperate *for a pianist for a group in Braintree. I adore the name. Very beneath me, R. said, but he'd be too grateful, and I do owe him some. So I'm off on the Greyhound at 11. I'll call you tonight.*

Entirely missing, Julian observes, is Karen's usual unspoken threat, the suicide blackmail. She sounds, one could almost say, lighthearted. However, it is annoying, still, on some levels. Annoying and more: Roger is or has been (probably) a love of Karen's, at least someone on whom she had a sort of crush. Also, Julian suspects that he is alcoholic. And usually broke.

Closer to the surface, there is the aborted plan for lunching in Portland. A tour of the new art museum, and the new waterfront development, both supposed to be handsome, innovative. But that excursion, Julian in a moment decides, is precisely what he will do. Portland by himself. Why not?

But first he will call and check on planes to San Francisco for tonight. With the time difference he can probably arrange to arrive fairly early in the evening.

He will go directly to Lila.

––––––––

"I do wonder what we'll do next, don't you?" It is Julian who has said this, to Lila, on the morning after his return from Maine. But even as Lila smiles at his phrasing, at the implication of their being watchers rather than participants, in fact protagonists, she reflects that it could have been she herself who spoke. She too wonders what will be next, for them. However, she only murmurs (somewhat falsely), "Do we have to do anything?"

They are still in bed, Lila's bed, in her fairly crowded bedroom (piles of books, too many clothes). Julian, still on Eastern time, Maine time, has awakened early, and Julian awake tends to be restive. Lila wishes that they could simply go back to sleep; this is surely not a moment for decisions, or plans.

This room, in the back of Lila's small house, has views only of trees, and ferns, all at the moment dripping with fog, nothing visible but leaves and fronds and fog, as though the house itself were suspended in a forest, a California maze of redwoods, eucalyptus.

"If Karen decides to stay away this time, as I quite think she might," now says Julian, very alert, "that will make a difference. With us. I mean, of course it will."

"Of course," echoes Lila.

At that, at her sleepy voice, he very gently laughs, reaching to touch her shoulder. He asks, "If I left now could you go back to sleep?"

"I doubt it." She gives it a moment's thought. "And I don't really want you to go. I must not be feeling very intelligent." ("Resistance," some part of her mind labels what she is feeling.)

"On the other hand," Julian persists, "Garrett's going has not made a great deal of difference to us."

"No." Of course she cannot go back to sleep, and of course he has to go on talking.

"It's odd how passive we both are," Julian next says. "We've waited for them to act. For Garrett and Karen to leave us. Do you think it's because we're the guilty parties? Or could it be connected to what we do?"

"The way we sit around listening all day, watching people? I suppose. Maybe."

"Or, more likely our passive characters chose that profession in the first place?"

"Julian, would you like some breakfast?"

He kisses her, soundly but somewhat hastily. "As a matter of fact, I'm quite starved. My Maine appetite, along with the time."

That cold and foggy California August is succeeded, as sometimes happens out there, by a warm and golden fall that lasts and lasts, until the dread word *drought* begins to be spoken in some quarters. Even November of that year is bright and soft, the nights just barely cool.

The predictions that Julian made on the morning after his return from Maine (the morning he couldn't stop talking, is how Lila remembers it)—all that has turned out to be true: Karen, in the course of various phone calls, has announced that she does plan to spend at least the winter in Boston. Roger is almost always away somewhere; she can use his place in Watertown, so handy to Cambridge where she has friends. She is working in Braintree. Could Julian send a few clothes? Julian does send clothes, being more or less used to doing just that, but he does not go back there to see how she really is, as he used to do. He tells her that he believes they should have a more formal separation, and Karen says, *Why?* but she does not disagree.

And none of this with Karen has much effect on Lila and Julian, their private connection with each other. They are together rather more than before, but not as much as might under the circumstances be expected. Both are busy and often tired at night, and they do live more or less at opposite ends of the Golden Gate Bridge.

Sometimes they go to the same parties, with mutual friends, other shrinks, some professors, their old mix—but then they always have. Lila Lewisohn and Julian Brownfield have always been known to be friends.

Garrett telephones to say that Phyllis is in therapy, and seems to be doing somewhat better. They have not had a dinner party for almost two months. He hopes that he and Lila will run into each other, at least. Somewhere.

An odd series of circumstances has increased Lila's patient load: a colleague's illness, a referral from a valued doctor friend. So Lila is working longer and harder than usual. And even when she is not actively with patients she finds her mind reverting to them, to their concerns, hardly ever to her own. Which was not always the case with her, she reflects. Some balances, she senses, have been shifted. And quite possibly high time that they should, she concludes.

On the whole she is fairly content with her life and her work, with Julian.

But she senses that he is not; he seems to push for change. She sometimes feels that he would welcome almost any change.

First he begins to argue that now, this year, he could go along on her annual January trip to Mexico.

And as soon as he has made this suggestion Lila knows that she really wants to go alone to Mexico, as she always has. She tries to explain. "I'm so used to thinking of it as time alone. You know? No patients or friends. No husband."

"No lover," Julian supplies, with a smile that indicates understanding, if not pleasure.

"No one I know," Lila puts it, very much wishing that he had not brought this up.

"Sometimes I feel terribly odd," Julian tells her, on a somewhat later occasion. "Much odder than usual, I mean. I feel inhabited by Karen, curiously. With you I sometimes feel as though I were Karen, and you were me. And I want to complain, as she did to me, that you only care for your patients."

"And of course in a sense you'd be quite right, as she was," Lila tells him, uneasily, for she has had the same sense of increased dependence on Julian's part, which she is not at all sure that she likes.

They are seated during this particular conversation in Lila's kitchen, where Julian is making dinner. It has been established between them that Julian likes cooking more than Lila does, possibly because he has done somewhat less of it, in his masculine life. In any case, salmon steaks and polenta, with an interesting salad.

Watching him, his long clever hands and worried eyes, his tired face, Lila has then a curious vision, which is of Julian with another woman. Someone younger, more beautiful and more needful than she, Lila, is (not so needful as Karen though, and not alcoholic). Lila sees this clearly, although she knows that Julian loves her very much.

Yes, she thinks, Julian will fall in love with this other woman, who needs his care, Julian the caretaker, the generous protector.

Lila wonders next, of course, just what will happen to her, along those lines. Another love affair, or affairs—or, could she possibly marry again?

And she smiles, having realized that as to her own future she has not the slightest idea.

The Wrong Mexico

There they are, lying just apart on pink-striped plastic mattresses: Julian Brownfield, a lean, tanned, fiftyish Marin County psychiatrist, and Helen Eustis, a trim, tennis-playing mother of four, a barely gray California blond. Helen is Julian's very new lady friend, and they have traveled together to this smooth white Mexican beach that curves beautifully around a bay of glittering blue-green water. In front of Helen and Julian, then, is white sand and the sea, behind them the very snazzy new German-built and -owned resort in which they are staying, the Margarita, which is mostly pink, whirls and curlicues of pink stucco, and vast areas of glass (unusual, so much glass in Mexico; these huge panes were imported from Germany). Each guest room has its own small patio, with flowers, and each room faces out to the sea, as Julian and Helen are facing out now, from their plastic.

A few yards behind the Margarita the jungle begins to rise, thick and mysterious, a rich, impenetrable mass of greens, every possible shade of green. Mountains of jungle, the start of a range that extends far north of this resort, almost all the way to Mexico City.

———

Out on the beach, Julian is wearing new trunks that he bought for this trip, khaki-colored with a dark blue stripe, conservatively cut; they are perhaps a fraction too large. Helen's suit is black, cut fashionably high up on her good firm thighs, maybe a little tight across her unfashionably large breasts. But Julian and Helen both look good. Seen among the other tourists scattered about that beach, other Americans, Germans, French, people of varying ages, varying degrees of health and conditions of weight, these two Californians are considerably above average, in terms of general attractiveness.

And the sand around their chairs is very white and smoothly groomed, the sea before them lovely, with its bright gentle waves that swell out to the distant horizon, where the bay is marked by graceful hills on either side, where each evening a new sunset silhouettes the fine-drawn black trees.

But everything is wrong with this picture.

Julian would say that if he could. He would say, Everything is wrong. Worse than in most of my patients' lives.

This is not even the resort that he meant to come to, an error compounded of other errors, almost impossible to explain and, worse, unrectifiable, probably.

To try to put it in order, to speak sensibly of what is senseless: Julian first heard of a Mexican resort from a woman named Lila Lewisohn, also a psychiatrist, and Julian's former colleague-friend-lover—Julian has no way of describing his present relation to Lila, and this in itself is a source of general terribleness, of mess. *Estranged* is the coldly accurate word that presents itself; they have been slipping apart for no clear reason ever since his divorce.

In any case, while she was married (while she was Julian's lover) Lila used to come each winter to Mexico, alone. She looked forward to Mexico all year; she spoke of butterflies and flowers, seafood and swimming. Some town with an Indian-sounding name, as this town has, on a bay. A name something like Margarita. However, there the descriptions parted: Lila's hotel was up on a bluff above the sea, whereas this one is emphatically at sea level. Lila's was old, slightly shabby, she said; this one is most garishly, horrifyingly new.

Has Julian come to Mexico in search of Lila, if unconsciously? And come to the wrong place, and with the wrong woman? All this seems quite possible to Julian, now.

His connection with Helen began with the initially innocent habit of fruit juice at a health bar, after tennis; they played at the same Mill Valley club. And a couple of times when Julian had no patients for an hour they went on to lunch. Sandwiches on the Sausalito waterfront, and pleasant talk. And this woman seemed so unshadowed, her life so simple and sunny, despite an alcoholic former husband, a divorce, that to Julian she was exotic. More usual in his life were the infinite troubles and suffering of patients, and his own infinitely troubled former wife, an alcoholic. Not to mention the complexities of love with Lila, who was intense and subtle, complicated. Julian was drawn to Helen, this generous-bodied woman (both he and Lila tended to be too thin). A blond who was sort of pretty.

Naturally enough, in the course of things, Helen invited Julian to her house for dinner, a nice big open redwood house, on Cloudview, in Sausalito. She barbecued chicken in her vine-sheltered patio, played Mozart, and poured a lot of good chardonnay. Nothing original, but all so nice, so reassuring to a man who lately had been feeling old and tired and cold, and almost sexless. And so in what seemed a natural way he and Helen went off to bed that night (her kids were all conveniently away with their father, now an A.A. success), and there Julian experienced a happy sensual exchange. It was nice.

And the next morning Helen said, "I've been wanting to go to Mexico. How about you?"

The only way to explain this to Lila (though "estranged" as lovers, they still talked a lot, mostly on the phone) was just to say that he was going to Mexico with a woman with whom he might, or well might not, be "in love"—or so he had insanely believed at the time. He now thinks that he could as easily and far more truthfully have said, I feel restless and sad, inadequate. I am middle aged, in crisis, and now this nice woman has asked me to go to Mexico with her. I am almost severely depressed.

He could surely have said all that (it would have explained their estrangement as well), but he did not. He said "possibly in love." And Lila, very hurt indeed, and angry, said, "Well, okay. And no, I don't particularly want to see you. No, we're not exactly friends."

And so, there is Julian, desperately missing Lila and certainly not in love with Helen, to whom he is utterly unable to make love. ("My cock is dead," a patient once memorably, terribly said to Julian.)

And there is Helen, who believed that she was going off on this sexy Mexican trip with a nice psychiatrist, finally a man she could talk to, a man who would listen and maybe tell her what to do.

Helen is worried about her children. That came out in their first night's conversation—somewhat drunken, at the bar. Something wrong in the kitchen, dinner was announced as late, and then later still.

Especially her oldest daughter worries Helen, a girl named

Robin, who Helen believes—well, she knows that Robin does drugs. And drinks too much. And has friends who steal cars; for all Helen knows Robin steals cars too.

"At the meetings they say detach. Detach with love. But how? And even if you really do the first step and admit you're powerless. You're still a parent. You can't really be sure you didn't cause it. I mean, Freud? And I don't really like the meetings, they make me feel old. All those kids going on about parents who drink. Robin used to go to the A.C.A. meetings herself. Her father's idea, but you can't exactly say it worked, I don't think."

At that point Helen's face had begun to blur, for Julian. "No," he said.

"Well, what do you really think, Julian? Do you think a regular old-fashioned psychoanalysis would do her any good?"

"Well. Well I don't really know."

Julian was feeling at that moment the infinite sadness of Robin. Rather drunkenly he thought, Poor Robin, and poor Helen, who he was sure was a very nice if somewhat mixed-up woman. And poor himself, he who had really fucked things up, bringing this nice woman to this awful place, and under pretenses that became more false with every tropical, sweaty minute. As false as the plastic birds-of-paradise behind all those glistening bar glasses—although for all he knew the horrible flowers were real.

The bar was open to the sea. Thus from high uncomfortable stools Helen and Julian were confronted with all that water, a dangerous, deathless black expanse, the sand before it gray and damp. And the night itself was damp, and hot, the air black and thick and heavy. The jungle might at any moment descend upon them, Julian felt, with all its myriad lurking dangers.

And the noise: a defective speaker system jolted out old sixties songs, Beatles and Stones and Beach Boys, all sounding exactly alike, all loud. And everyone else in the bar, all those other hungry guests were more and more drunkenly, loudly talk-ing. Arguing. Shouting.

It was hardly the time or place for Julian to give out a professional opinion, even had he had one. He knew nothing whatsoever—least of all about himself, and why he had made this incomprehensible journey, with a woman who was not and would not turn into Lila.

Years ago Karen, to whom Julian was married, used to make fun of Lila's trips to Mexico. "I personally hate the very idea of Mexico," Karen said. "Dirty. Everyone so poor that you have to feel guilty all the time. I hate countries like that; you couldn't pay me to go down there. Yuck!"

And how idyllic now even those bad old days with Karen seemed; even then there was always the refuge of Lila. Of love.

And so why, after Lila's divorce, and then Julian's, did they begin to see each other less, rather than the more often that might have been expected? Why did they allow themselves to "drift apart"?

Because we were both too tired to make a commitment, has been one answer.

Or because we had got so used to being married to others, to illicit love.

Or (now thought Julian) because I was gradually going into a depression, into this depression.

Now the sea like the jungle seemed to threaten. Julian imag-ined huge sudden walls of waves, engulfing, overwhelming. He shivered, terrified.

"You can't be cold?" Good, maternal Helen. "Darling, you're not coming down with something bad?"

How dare she call him darling? Julian irrationally thought that. And yet he did think it: *How dare she?*

The dinner that was served at last was, as everyone in one way or another remarked, not worth waiting for. Pale under-cooked fish and canned peas. "I don't think I've had canned peas since college," was Helen's remarkable pleasant comment. She was trying; heaven knows she was trying.

From dinner they went immediately to bed. What else? And there they both tried hard, tried for love and ease and simple sat-isfaction. But nothing worked, no gesture or effort on either of their parts. (*My cock is dead.* Julian thought of saying that, a last desperate wild effort at something like a joke. But did not.) And poor Helen probably felt that it was all her fault, despite all the good advice she was getting at those meetings: you didn't cause, you can't cure.

Together they pushed the coarse sheets back from their sweaty bodies, and tried to sleep.

The next day was very much the same as that one. Bright talk at breakfast, Helen being jocular about the other guests. And then they went out to the beach chairs, the glaring sand, and the too-bright sea.

Helen swam a lot, and surely, Julian hoped, that part of this nightmare trip was good for her, a pleasure? He sat heavily on his chair while she swam. Rooted. Too heavy to move, although in fact he was losing weight, was visibly too thin. But he was too heavy to swim, he felt. His head would weigh him down.

Julian diagnosed himself: this is at least a medium-severe depression. And he made his recommendations: work on fight-ing it off, do not just sit around and let it get worse.

But he did nothing of the sort. He did nothing.

And now, like a large slick blond sea creature, Helen comes back from the ocean, walking across the stretch of beach to Julian's chair. Helen, gingerly stepping, the sand must be terrifi-cally hot. Sitting down she winces at the contact with hot plastic. Then she smiles and tosses her long wet hair. "It feels great," she says. "You really should try it."

"I know."

"I was talking to a woman out there about Oaxaca," Helen then tells him. "She says you can get a small plane from here and I've always wanted to go there."

Does she really imagine that he can take still another Mexican trip? Surely not. "Oaxaca," Julian repeats, heavily separating the unfamiliar syllables.

Amazingly, surprising him utterly, Helen then laughs. "Come on, I know you don't want to go there. Why don't you come along in a couple of days if you feel like it? And if not, not. I'll see you back in California."

Searching her face for strain, or some falsehood, Julian finds neither: this good woman really wants to go to Oaxaca, and she has decided to leave him alone.

And so, miraculously, Helen packs for the afternoon plane, the small one to Oaxaca. "I sort of think you need to be by yourself for a while," she murmurs, kissing him good-bye up near the front desk. No point in his coming to the airport, Helen says.

Left alone, Julian feels—not exactly better, but just slightly less heavy, the burden of Helen gone, and the even greater burden of pretending to be all right.

But how incredibly nice she was, after all. She did in fact manage to detach with love. What a kind and understanding woman. Sane. Her daughter will be all right, probably, eventually, Julian thinks. She's just being an adolescent in Marin County, in the terrible late eighties. He should have said something of the sort to Helen, Julian thinks, and he determines that he will do so on his return to California.

And with that determination Julian reaches several conclusions. One (no doubt this was obvious all along, to Helen too), he has no intention of going on to Oaxaca. He will fly back to Mexico City and then on to San Francisco, where his car is. Where Lila is.

And, two, even that tiny bit of professional thought, of work, about Helen's child has made him feel the tiniest bit better.

Among Julian's professional colleagues, local psychiatrists and psychoanalysts, three men in the past two years have committed suicide, in severe depressions. And the overall suicide rate for shrinks is not encouraging; in fact it is terrifying to Julian, a depressed psychiatrist.

What laymen say about shrinks is largely true, he believes. We're all nuts.

And in panic he thinks, I have got to get out of this. (It is unclear to Julian whether he means out of Mexico or out of his depression: out of both, probably.)

And so Julian makes an effort, a desperate effort, in fact, to treat himself as a patient, to be gentle and understanding and at the same time firm, making certain demands. The good-parent model. And to do as he often tells patients to do: exercise, almost any activity is preferable to doing nothing.

Walking along the beach, as he begins that afternoon to force himself to do, he observes that the jungle hills are at their lowest just behind his hotel. Farther along, small overgrown ridges rise up from the edge of the beach, a tamed area of jungle. There are even a few small houses and civilized paths. Palm trees, climbing bougainvillea, in marvelous shades of pink-red-purple.

If Lila would "take him back" he would be instantly all right, thinks Julian the patient.

If they could be lovers again, he and Lila, he would be okay, or nearly, thinks almost totally irrational, almost helpless Julian.

All of which wise Julian the therapist knows to be untrue.

The calves of his legs have begun to ache from trudging through the sand, and so Julian heads down to the edge of the water— where, he observes, looking downward, the small waves have left lovely and complicated patterns, curves upon curves, on the dark wet packed sand. Ridiculous sandpipers run along there, rushing suddenly inland, as though they had never seen a wave before.

That night from the bar and later from his solitary room Julian can see strings of lights from a cruise ship anchored out there in the harbor: false glamour on false masts, thinks Julian, sourly. Love boats.

And the next day, as despite sore legs he forces himself to walk again, the beach is all taken up, crowded with what must be people from that boat, in their bright cruise clothes, their Frisbees and cameras.

To avoid those crowds, he begins to walk at the upper edge of the beach, the jungle edge, except that he has come to a place that is relatively cultivated, bougainvillea streaming in vines and bursts of bloom, and a path that leads upward. A path that on a random impulse Julian takes, and climbs. Although it is not very steep he is forced to stop several times to breathe, as he thinks, I'm not in the greatest shape, I'm really not.

But each step affords a new view, immediately of flowers and hummingbirds, and butterflies, small and yellow among the profusion of petals—and, farther out, a new glimpse of the sea, just now in all its brilliant midday glitter. Then as he climbs on, a giant clump of coconut palms obscures his view, waving thick green fronds, gray trunks that very slightly sway in a fresh new morning breeze.

At the top, the first structure that Julian sees is a sort of wooden platform, over at the farther edge of this small cliff. A platform whose sides are roped off from the precipice. A place that Julian has heard described by Lila. Quite clearly he hears her voice as she tells him, as she has told him, "The bar is quite wonderful, although I don't spend a lot of time there. It's very glamorous; you look down at the sea and the sand through all those palm trees."

And he hears himself: "Couldn't I come down there with you? Or if not with, at the same time you go?" Pleadingly.

"But that would be with, Julian darling." And her laugh.

Magically, as in a fairy tale, he has come to Lila's place—and how very beautiful it is. Just as she said. How very unlike where Julian has been, the low-down swamp-level Margarita. Straightening up, standing as tall as he can, Julian breathes the new air. The higher, clearer air. Although the thirty or forty feet that he judges the bluff to be should not make a difference in the air, it does.

Closing his eyes for a minute, Julian thinks that if this were indeed a fairy story, Lila would at this moment magically appear. Lila, forgiving all. Recalled to love, magically.

Opening his eyes Julian sees, of course, no one. No one whatsoever. In a desultory way he begins to walk about, over toward the bar and then toward a blue plaster structure: steps, pillars, a porch open to some very large rooms beyond. All quite deserted, and Julian sees then that no one has been around for quite a while, that Lila's retreat is now defunct, in the process of being swallowed by the jungle. Heavy encroaching vines are now in charge. Vines have almost closed off windows and pulled down a corner of the roof. A deserted place, dead. But as Julian thinks that, *dead,* he sees a tiny quick bright lizard flash across the blue plaster and vanish into a crack.

This is something to telephone Lila about, Julian boyishly, idiotically thinks. An excuse to call her.

"Oh yes," says the youthful German owner-manager of the Margarita, that night at the bar. "Once a place possessed of a certain charm. Quaint." Hugo is proud of his English, learned at Stanford. "First built by Mexicans, and, you know how that goes. And then owned by certain not-attractive compatriots of my own. There were scandals concerning certain contraband substances. And then a charming Mexican fellow managed to buy them out, quite competent as an owner, I believe. But a Swedish wife who made perpetual trouble. As a combination impossible, a Mexican and a Swedish. Imagine yourself. In any case as you see now quite finished. An eyesore you might say."

Julian, who has put in a call to Lila, in San Francisco, has found the sheer length of this spiel quite intolerable. He stares at the wall phone, that small black instrument of torture. His enemy. The perfect objective correlative for his angst. Already it has rung twice, loud sudden bursts to which Hugo has responded in shouted German—for so long! so that now, as Hugo goes on and on with his gossip, Julian stares malevolently, hopelessly at the black plastic shape, until it distorts, becoming a giant spider on the wall.

It has occurred to Julian, too, that all that he will have to say to Lila will necessarily be also for the large ears of Hugo, and he imagines how Hugo later can tell the story: the crazy man who came there, an American, a *psychiatrist* (all the funnier, everyone

knows that shrinks are very funny). The crazy man who came
there with a woman whom he then sent away, although she was
a blond and quite attractive, for her age.

But what then? How will the story finish off? Julian has no
clear idea, none at all, about what to say to Lila. About what
to do.

"Although there is a rumor that a certain relative of Señor de
la Madrid has an interest in that location," Hugo more or less
winds up, and then is mercifully summoned to the kitchen by a
beckoning waiter.

At which moment the phone begins to ring, shrill and far
more loudly than before. Or so it seems to Julian.

Anxious, in fact desperate to stop that sound, though once
more certain that the call will not be his, Julian picks up the
receiver, into which he says, "Hello." He can hear a lot of indis-
tinguishable background noise.

A high-pitched voice comes on, speaking in Spanish, of
which Julian understands very little. He is about to call out for
Hugo when he clearly makes out the words, "Estados Unidos"
and then, "San Francisco." As loudly and clearly as he can he
shouts into the receiver, "Sí! Sí . . . Sí!"

A silence follows, broken only by various small mechanical
sounds, all to Julian ominous.

But then there is the very distinct ringing of a phone, Lila's
phone (it must be Lila's) in the house in San Francisco. An
empty house; it has that sound, and Julian's heart too feels
empty, vacant, hollowed out.

Then: "This is Dr. Lewisohn. I will be in my office tomorrow
at 8:30. If you wish me to call you before that, please leave your
name and telephone number."

Beep.

With no idea whatsoever what to say—he had not thought of
her answering machine as a possibility—Julian starts in anyway.
"Lila it's me. I'm in Mexico. I think I've been sick. I mean a

depression. Crisis time. What I told you wasn't exactly true; I'm here by myself. I'll explain all that but it's not important. And I think I must have come here looking for you, but it's not the right place, and I think I found your place, but it looks all closed. This place is horrible; it's called the Margarita. Lila, just talking to you, you can't imagine—" Out of breath, and afraid that his voice will break, Julian pauses, and then hears again, Beep.

He considers placing another call, but what would he say? Does she need to hear further explanations? "I was with someone here, a perfectly nice woman, just an awful mistake. In fact horrible white nights and a couple of terrible days that wouldn't end. So she left. I'm trying to treat myself for a bad depression and in a way I think I'm doing fairly well." Not exactly a message to place between beeps, even assuming that he could get her number again. The answering machine of Dr. Lewisohn.

"How very fortunate to have after all a call that comes through. So often not the case," pronounces Hugo, returned to Julian's side at the bar. How long had he been there? Heard how much? Julian has no idea. "Mexicans," Hugo continues. "A lovely people, very gentle, but not gifted in things mechanical."

"I think I'll go along to bed now," Julian tells him.

It is only when he is lying in bed and wondering if he will ever sleep that Julian remembers that he has skipped dinner. He did not even think of dinner.

An hour or so later he is wrestling with the idea of a sleeping pill. On general principles he resists, when he can. However, a 15

Dalmane would at least give him a couple of hours, and probably spare him several hours of this ghastly wakefulness.

With Helen, Julian took breakfast in his room, their room. But today, as though to emphasize his new status as a person alone, he orders coffee and rolls in the bar (where the telephone is).

A strange day. The sky is a curious yellow, hazed over, but the lifeless air is still extremely hot, and no breeze disturbs the green glass Pacific. Despite this uninviting weather the beach looks more crowded than usual, even—not with love-boat tourists in their terrible bright clothes but with Mexican families, dark plump young mothers and round brown babies, thin strutting young men and boys, now in full possession. They have now reclaimed the land for their own, as it surely should be—as the vines and flowers have reclaimed the place that used to be Lila's private resort. Still semidrugged, romantically Julian thinks, Ah, good.

"Sunday," Hugo sighs, on his way through the bar, having uninvitedly paused at Julian's table. "They come like flies, all the villagers. As though the beach were theirs."

"Well isn't it, really?"

Hugo frowns. "Well in a strange quite antediluvian way you are correct. The rights of Indians. Property laws, quite obscure but on occasion still invoked." He sighs again, and even more hatefully asks, "You again await a phone call?"

"More or less."

By noon, though, after several hot and distractingly noisy hours, on his single mattress, Julian is not at all certain just what it is that he waits for. He has begun to suspect that it is the arrival of Lila herself that in some part of his disordered mind he anticipates. She must know how he needs her!

At each sound of traffic, of taxi horns, slammed car doors, Julian imagines that it is in fact Lila, simply there, and he thinks, If she would just *arrive* we could simply be here together. Swim and take walks, for a while not talk. Perhaps eventually make love.

However, disturbed as he is, "not himself," Julian is able to recognize the impossibility of this particular fantasy, to see how unlikely that Lila, having heard his confused and very partial "explanation" on her answering machine (her *machine*, for God's sake) would pack up and take off for Mexico. As though he were sick, a patient who had to be rescued.

It is utterly out of the question for Lila to just show up, he thinks. But how I long for her to do so.

And there he is on the beach, on his pink-striped mattress. Pinioned there by his own crazy expectations. This must be one of the ways in which women suffer, Julian thinks. This terrible waiting for phone calls, or arrivals. This desperate passivity. How do they stand it? he wonders.

He forces himself to walk down at least to the edge of the water (where Hugo could easily see him) and then to walk for a while along the sand.

Viewed from close up, the Mexican families do not look so round and smiley as earlier he had imagined. They look like very poor people out for a brief and rather meager excursion, on someone else's beach. Hugo's beach.

In a more just world, thinks Julian, returning from a longer walk than he intended—he managed to force himself along—he should now be rewarded by at least some sign from Lila; if not herself, then a telephone message, a cable. Fax. Whatever people send these days.

And indeed as he approaches the bar he sees Hugo there, gesturing in his direction. Julian hurries toward him.

But, "I have just to receive a cancellation," Hugo tells him, eagerly. "And I thought perhaps you prolong your stay? A week more?"

"Oh Christ. I mean no. No thanks."

Going to the bar, Julian desperately orders a margarita.

He should, he thinks, make plans to fly home tomorrow. However, since he arranged (before this lunatic trip) to see no patients for another week, that means seven days alone in Mill Valley. Trying to pull himself together and get some sleep. Trying not to jump off the bridge. Trying not to call Lila.

He stares with horror at the plastic birds-of-paradise on the bar, and at the fat blond couple from Texas who are necking in a darkened corner of the room.

Sipping at his very strong, sweet drink, though, Julian notes that it is making him feel the very slightest shade better. It might even be possible to eat some dinner, later on, and to tell Hugo to telephone about his tickets. But the face he sees, his own, reflected in the mirror above the bar looks seriously disordered. Pale, unbalanced: the clinician within him makes that judgment.

Not the best time to take to drink, thinks normally abstemious Julian.

And then the phone rings. Julian watches as Hugo picks up the receiver. "Allo? Allo?" And then beckons to Julian, grimacing his version of a smile, as Julian wonders: Is this some cruel joke? Is he drunk?

"Hello, Julian, is that you?"

At the clear familiar sound of Lila's voice Julian feels not drunk at all; he feels almost sane (though with some fear that he might cry). He says only, "Lila—"

"So there you are. Why on earth the Margarita? I could have told you it was awful."

"But Lila—" Not saying, But we were not exactly trading travel plans, Julian instead tries to laugh.

"Your message didn't sound so good, but now you sound better."

"Well, that's true. I mean I haven't been in great shape, but now I've been walking, some swimming—"

"Well, that's good. My own prescriptions." She laughs, a sound that seems to fade in and out.

"But I think I'll fly back tomorrow, stay home for a week. Do some reading." Saying this though Julian recognizes a bleak and bad idea.

As does Lila, apparently. "Why not stay down there a little more? Really swim, walk farther. It might do you some good."

Wild hope leaps in Julian's blood. "But would you—? Could you come—"

Very gently she tells him, "No, I really can't get away right now. But you'll be okay, I know." Meaning: you know how to cure yourself, and you can.

"Yes," Julian tells her. And he manages not to say, Will you marry me? When I come back can we move in together? He only says, "I'll see you in San Francisco?"

What he meant as a statement has emerged as a question, and Lila answers, "Yes, of course," very warmly. And then she says, "You could do me a favor, sort of. Walk over to my place again, and really check it out. Find out anything you can."

"Oh sure. Of course. And I think you're right about a little longer here. But I do wish—I wish you—"

"So do I, but I can't. You'll be okay though."

"I know."

"Well—"

They say good-bye, and although the last thing he really wants is the rest of his drink, Julian heads back to the bar.

He is intercepted right off by Hugo though, who jauntily

tells him, "Last chance! I go now to offer the room to a bureau of travel."

"Oh. Well as a matter of fact I do need the room after all. For myself."

"Ah good! You learn to like our beaches and our life down here?"

"More or less," Julian tells him. "I mean, more and more." Having intended some small irony, the tiniest joke, he is somewhat surprised at Hugo's enthusiastic response.

"So good! And then perhaps you come here every year," says Hugo.

"I really very much doubt that," Julian tells him. And then, more gently, "But of course it's entirely possible."

"Very good! And now I buy you a drink. Yes, doctor, I insist! It is not so often that I have psychiatrists for guests."

Earthquake Damage

Stretching long legs to brace her boots against the bulkhead as the plane heads upward from Toronto into gray mid-October air, Lila Lewisohn, a very tall, exhausted psychiatrist—a week of meetings has almost done her in, she feels—takes note of the advantages of this seat: enough leg room, and somewhat out of the crush. Also, the seat next to hers is vacant. At least, she thinks, the trip will be comfortable; maybe I can sleep.

But a few minutes into the air the plane is gripped and shaken. Turbulence rattles everything, as passengers clutch their armrests, or neighboring human arms, if they are traveling with friends or lovers. Lila, for whom this is a rather isolated period, instead grips her own knees, and grits her teeth, and prays—to no one, or perhaps to a very odd bunch: to God, in whom she does not believe; to Freud, about whom she has serious doubts; to her old shrink, who is dead; to her mother, also dead, and whom she mostly did not like. And to her former (she supposes it is now former) lover, Julian Brownfield, also a shrink.

Lila and Julian, in training together in Boston, plunged more or less inadvertently from a collegial friendship into heady adulterous love—a love (and a friendship) that for many years worked, sustaining them both through problematic marriages. But in the five or six years since the dissolutions of those marriages a certain troubled imbalance has set in. Most recently, Julian has taken back his ex-wife, Karen, an alcoholic pianist who is not doing well with recovery and has just violently separated from another husband. *Sheltering* might be Julian's word for what he is doing for Karen—Lila would call it *harboring,* or worse: if Karen behaved well, she might stay on forever there with Julian, Lila at least half believes. She has so far refused to see Julian, with Karen there.

In any case, Lila now prays to all those on her list, and especially to Julian, to whom she says, I'm just not up to all this; I'm really running on empty. *Please.*

Her meetings, held in the new Harbourfront section of Toronto, in an excellent hotel with lovely, wide lake views, were no more than routinely tiring, actually; Lila was forced to admit to herself that it was the theme of the conference that afflicted her with a variety of troubled feelings. It was a psychiatric conference on the contemporary state of being single, though of course certain newspaper articles vulgarized it into "A New Look at Singles," "Singles: Shrinks Say the New Minority." Whereas in fact the hours of papers and discussion had ranged about—had included the guilt that many people feel over their single state; social ostracism, subtle and overt; myths of singleness; the couple as conspiracy; plus practical problems, demographics, and perceived changes over the last several generations. And Lila found that she overreacted—she was reached, touched, shaken by much that was said. She had trouble sleeping, despite long lap swims in the hotel's glassed-in pool, with its views of Canadian skies across Lake Ontario.

Now, very tired, she braces herself against the turbulence, and against certain strong old demons in her mind. And then, as though one of those to whom she has prayed were indeed in charge, the turbulence ends. The huge plane zooms peacefully through a clear gray dusk. Westward, toward San Francisco. A direct flight.

Lila must have fallen asleep, for she is startled awake by the too loud voice of the pilot, over the intercom: "Sorry, folks. We've just had news of a very mild earthquake in the San Francisco area, very mild but a little damage to the airport, so we'll be heading back to Toronto."

An instant of silence is followed by loud groans from the rows and rows of seats behind Lila's bulkhead. Groans and exclamations: *Oh no, Jesus Christ, all we need, an earthquake.* Turning, she sees that a great many people are standing up, moving about, as if there were anything to do. One man, though—trench-coated, lean, dark blond, almost handsome—makes for the telephone up on the wall near Lila's seat. Seizing it, he begins to dial, and dial and dial. Lila gestures that he can sit down in the empty seat, and he does so, with a twisting grimace. Then, "Can't get through, *damn,*" he says. "My family's down on the Peninsula." He dials again, says, "Damn," again, then asks Lila, "Yours?"

"Oh. Uh, San Francisco."

"Well, San Francisco's better. Guy with a radio said the epi-center's in Hollister."

"I wonder about that 'mild.' " Lila leans toward him to whisper.

"No way it could be mild. They're not closing down the air-port for any mild earthquake."

Which is pretty much what Lila had already thought.

"Well, I guess I better let someone else try to phone."

"There's one on the other side," Lila tells him, having noticed this symmetrical arrangement on entering the plane.

"Oh, well then." But after a few minutes, muttering, he gets up and goes back to his seat, as Lila realizes that she wishes he had stuck around—not that she was especially drawn to him; she simply wanted someone there.

People are by now crowding around the two phones, pressing into the passageway between the aisles. A man has managed to get through to his sister-in-law, in Sacramento, and soon everyone has his news: it is a major quake. Many dead. The bridge down.

At that last piece of news, about the bridge, Lila's tired heart is drenched with cold, as she thinks: Julian. Julian, who lives in Mill Valley and practices in San Francisco, could be on the bridge at any time. Especially now, just after five in San Francisco. Commuter time.

On the other hand, almost anyone *could* have been on the bridge, especially anyone who lives in Marin County. Fighting panic, Lila says this firmly to herself: anyone does not mean Julian, necessarily. A major disaster involving the bridge does not necessarily involve Julian Brownfield. Not necessarily. She is gripping her knees, as during the turbulence; with an effort she unclenches her fingers and clasps her hands together on her lap, too tightly.

"How about the game?" someone near her is saying.

"No stadium damage, I heard."

"Lucky it wasn't a little later. People leaving, going back to Oakland."

As, very slowly, these sentences penetrate Lila's miasma of anxiety, she understands: they are talking about the Bay Bridge. The Bay Bridge was damaged, not the Golden Gate. Traffic to the East Bay, not to Marin, Mill Valley.

What Lila feels then, along with extreme relief, is an increase of exhaustion; her nerves sag. And she has, too, the cold new thought that Julian, an unlikely fan, could well have gone to the game. (Taken Karen to the game?) Could have left early, and been overtaken by the earthquake, anywhere at all.

Rising from her seat, intending to walk about, she sees that everyone else is also trying to move. They all seem to protest the event, and their situations, with restless, random motion. Strangers confront and query each other along the packed aisles: Where're you from? Remember the quake last August? The one in '72? In '57? How long were you in Toronto? Like it there? But not enough to make you want to go back right away, right?

At last they begin the descent into Toronto, strapped in, looking down, and no one notices the turbulence that they pass through.

In Julian's house, high up on the wooded crest above Mill Valley, there is total chaos: in the front hall, two large suitcases lie open and overflowing—a crazy tangle of dresses and blouses, sweaters, silk nightgowns, pantyhose, and shoes thrown all over.

"Anyone coming in," Julian comments from a doorway, "anyone would think the earthquake, whereas actually—"

"Well, in a way it is the fucking earthquake," Karen unnecessarily tells him, in her furious, choppy way. "Closing the fucking airport."

"Whereas, really, we were lucky," Julian continues, more or less to himself. He is tall and too thin, gray-haired. His skin, too, now looks gray: three weeks of Karen have almost done him in, he thinks. In character, she has alternated her wish to leave with a passionate desire to stay with Julian—forever. Only a day ago she had decided firmly (it seemed) to leave. And now, on the verge of her departure, an earthquake. "The airport might open in a couple of hours," Julian tells Karen, and he is thinking of Lila, the exact hour of whose return he is uncertain about. Perhaps she is already here? "Or tomorrow," he says to Karen, hopefully.

"But how would we know, with the phone out?" Karen complains. "It might be a couple of weeks." She is visibly at the end of her rope, which is short at the best of times. "A couple of weeks with no lights or electricity!"

It is clear to Julian that whatever controls Karen has managed to place on herself for the course of her stay are now wavering, if not completely gone. She has not behaved badly; she has not, that is, got drunk. He himself, at this moment, acutely longs for a drink. An odd longing: Julian is generally abstemious, a tennis player, always in shape. And he wonders, is he catching Karen's own longing, her alcoholic impulse? Karen, opposing A.A. (she did not like it there), believes that alcoholics can cut down, citing herself as an example—every night she has one, and only one, vodka martini.

Karen is very beautiful, still. All that booze has in no way afflicted the fine white skin. Her face shows no tracks of pain, nor shadows. Her wide, dark-blue eyes are clear; looking into those eyes, one might imagine that her head resounds only with Mozart, or Brahms—and perhaps in a way it still does.

"Well, come on, Julian, let's find some candles. You know perfectly well that this is the cocktail hour," she says to her former husband, and she laughs.

Down on the ground in Toronto, disembarked, all the passengers from the flight to San Francisco are herded into a room where, they are assured, they will be given instructions. And in that large, bare room rumors quickly begin to circulate, as people gather and mutter questions to each other.

No one is sitting or standing alone, Lila notices, although surely there were other solitary travelers on that plane. And she finds that she, too, begins to attach herself to groups, one after another. Is she seeking information, or simple creature comfort, animal reassurance? She is not sure.

Three businessmen in overcoats, with lavish attaché cases, having spoken to the pilot, inform Lila that it may be several days before the San Francisco airport opens. And that the reason for not going on to L.A., or even to Reno or Salt Lake City, has to do with flight regulations—since theirs was a Canadian carrier, they had to return to Canada.

In an automatic way she looks across to the man in the trench coat, at the same time wondering why: Why has she more or less chosen him to lead her? She very much doubts that it is because he is almost handsome, and she hopes that it is not simply that he is a man. He looks decisive, she more or less concludes, and then is shaken by a powerful memory of Julian, who is neither handsome nor decisive, and whom she has loved for all those years.

The trench-coated man seems indeed to have a definite group of his own, of which he is in charge. Lila reads this from the posture of the four people whom she now approaches, leaving the didactic businessmen. But before Lila can ask anything, the loudspeaker comes on, and a voice says that they are all to be housed in the Toronto Hilton, which is very near, and that the airline will do everything possible to get them to their destination tomorrow. A van will pick them up downstairs to take them to the hotel. Names will be called, vouchers given.

Lila has barely joined her chosen group when she hears her name called; they must be doing it by rows, she decides. She is instructed to go through a hall and down some stairs, go outside, and meet the Hilton van there.

And after a couple of wrong turns Lila indeed finds herself outside in the semidark, next to a dimly lit, low-ceilinged traffic tunnel, where a van soon does arrive. But it is for the Ramada Inn, not the Hilton.

And that is the last vehicle of any nature to show up for the next ten or twelve minutes, during which time no people show up, either. No one.

Several taxis are parked some yards down from where Lila has been standing, pacing, in her boots, by her carry-on bag.

Drivers are lounging on the seats inside. Should she take a cab to the Hilton? On the other hand, maybe by now everything has been changed, and no one is going to the Hilton after all.

It is very cold, standing there in the dark tunnel, and seemingly darker and dingier all the time. Across the black, wide car lanes are some glassed-in offices, closed and black, reflecting nothing. Behind Lila is the last room through which she came. It is still lit, and empty.

Something clearly is wrong; things cannot be going as planned. Or, she is in the wrong place. Then, dimly, at the end of the tunnel, she sees a van moving toward her. It will not be a Hilton van, she thinks, and she is right: HOLIDAY INN, its sign reads. It passes her slowly, an empty van, its driver barely looking out.

Lila is later to think of this period of time as the worst of the earthquake for her—a time in which she feels most utterly alone, quite possibly abandoned. It is so bad that she has forgotten about the earthquake itself almost entirely; she is too immediately frightened and uncomfortable to think of distant disaster.

After perhaps another five minutes, during which everything gets worse—the cold and the darkness, Lila's anxiety and her growing hunger—she hears voices from the room behind her. Turning, she sees what she thinks of as her group: the trench-coated man and his charges, followed by the other passengers, all coming out to where Lila stands, shifting her feet in boots that no longer seem to fit.

As though they were old friends, Lila hurries toward him. "Where've you been? What happened?"

"Bureaucratic foul-up," he tells her. "Some stuff about whether or not the airline would spring for the hotel. Who cares? And some confusion about whose flights originated in Toronto." With a semismile he adds, "You were really lucky to get out first."

"Was I? I don't know."

"Anyway. Look, there's our van. Toronto Hilton."

In the candlelit kitchen of Julian's house, Julian and Karen are drinking vodka and orange juice, Karen's idea being that they have to use up the orange juice before it goes to waste in the powerless refrigerator. "Besides, the C makes it good for you." She laughs, and Julian hears a sad echo of her old flirtatiousness as she adds, "But why am I telling a doctor anything like that?"

He sighs. "Yes, I am a doctor."

This is not a room designed for such romantic illumination. The shadows on the giant steel refrigerator are severe, menacing, and the flickering candlelight on the black-tiled floor looks evil—they could be in jail. Julian feels nothing of the vodka, and Karen's face, across the round, white, high-gloss table, shows mostly fatigue. She looks vague, distracted.

In a sober, conversational voice she remarks, "Funny to think back to old times in this kitchen. With Lila and old Garrett." Garrett: Lila's former husband, a mean and somber lawyer.

"This kitchen?" asks Julian. "I don't remember . . ."

"Sure you do. We were all drinking champagne, and later I broke a glass."

"I think it's Lila's kitchen we were in." The whole scene has indeed come back to Julian, a flash, immobilized: the other kitchen, so unlike this one, all soft wood, some copper bowls, blue pillows on a bench. Prim, pale Garrett—and Lila, her gray hair bright, brushed upward. Lila laughing and talking, he (Julian) talking, each of them, as always, excited by the other's sheer proximity. "It was somebody's birthday," he tells Karen, knowing perfectly well that it was Lila's. "You had on a green dress."

"Well, you sure do have a great memory for details."

"I have to, it's my job." And you always broke glasses, he does not say.

"You mean, my green dress is what you might call a professional memory? Holy shit, Julian, holy shit, you're, you're . . ." She begins to cough, unable to tell Julian what he is. He gets up and moves to pat her back, but Karen gestures him away.

"Don't, I'm okay, don't hit me!" She laughs a little hysterically, as Julian, too late, realizes that she is getting drunk. Is drunk. "You know what the earthquake was like for me?" She is looking blearily across at him, tears pooled in those great, dark-blue eyes. "*Fun.* The most fun in the world. I loved it."

"Good, Karen, I'm glad." It no longer matters what he says, Julian knows, as long as it is fairly neutral. "I thought it was more like turbulence in an airplane," he mutters, more or less to himself.

At which Karen giggles. "I like turbulence," she tells him. "Remember? I think it's a kick." And then, quite suddenly, she bursts into tears. "Julian, I've never loved anyone but you," she sobs, reaching out to him. Blindly.

Descending from the van at the Toronto Hilton, Lila and her new friends see that the lobby inside is very crowded. Everyone is gathered around a single small television screen, and in a room beyond there is a coffee shop, apparently open. "Hundreds killed," the announcer is saying. "Devastation."

"The restaurant's out of food," someone says.

There is a line at the reception desk, but it seems to move quickly; within minutes Lila is being assigned a room. "I wonder about phoning," she says to the man in the trench coat, Mark. They have all introduced themselves.

Lila's room, at the top of the Toronto Hilton, is actually a small suite, to which she pays no attention as she heads for the phone. Without considering consequences (Karen could easily answer), she dials the familiar Mill Valley number. Dialing directly, not bothering with credit cards or operators, she gets at first a busy signal and then an operator saying that she is sorry, all the circuits are busy. Lila dials again, gets more operators who are sorry, more busy signals. She goes into the bathroom to wash up, comes back and dials the number again, and again. She orders a sandwich from room service, and continues to try to phone.

A couple of hours later, in Mill Valley, Julian awakes with a sudden jolt: he is in his kitchen, still, and every brilliant light in the room is on, as is the television. Bottles and sticky glasses on the table. Gradually he remembers carrying Karen into the guest room. She is light enough in his arms, but a total dead weight; his back feels strained. And then he came back into this room. Surely not, he hopes, for another drink?

The TV screen shows a very large, white apartment building that has buckled and is rent with cracks and gaps. A background of black night sky, and a cordon of police. Cars, flashing lights. Dazed people standing around in clumps. Julian gets up to turn it off when, at that moment, the phone rings. In his confusion, he stumbles, just catches it on the third ring.

"Lila? My darling, my Lila, wherever . . . ? We're here, I mean I'm here, no damage, really. Well, I imagine I do sound odd, but no, of course I'm not drunk. Karen was just on the point of leaving—actually packed, then the damn thing hit. I guess she'll go tomorrow; by now I suppose I mean today. And you? You'll be back today! For sure?"

Smiling, still breathing hard with the effort of so much futile dialing before at last getting through, Lila offers a silent prayer to all those on her curious private list: she prays that she can fly out of Toronto tomorrow, or whatever day this now is—and that Karen can fly, finally, out of San Francisco.

She sleeps fitfully and wakes early, knowing that she is awake for good. She thinks of telephoning Julian again, but does not. She showers and dresses as hurriedly as possible, and goes down to the hotel lobby.

There people are sitting around, or milling about, aimlessly. The TV seems still to be showing the news from the night before; Lila glimpses the same bridge shots, fire shots, the broken apartment house. All around her in the lobby the faces are pale, clothes a little disheveled, as hers must be. From a small, plump woman who is sitting near the front desk she hears, "They say we're getting out today, but I don't believe it."

Lila, too, has trouble believing that they will escape. As she looks around at the tired clusters of people—no one, she observes again, is going it alone—she imagines that they will be there for months, that they are in fact refugees from some much larger disaster.

In the coffee shop, she finds Mark, and another man, and joins them. Mark got through to his wife, in Saratoga, who said that their chimney had fallen off, and that everything in the house that could break was broken. "But she's okay," says Mark, with a grin. "And the kids. You should have seen the waves in the swimming pool, she told me. You wouldn't believe it. Tidal."

From the lobby then, at first indistinctly, they hear an announcement: ". . . vans will begin to leave this hotel at nine-forty-five. Repeat: the San Francisco airport is clear."

Lila's seat on the morning plane is not nearly as good as the one the day before. Pushing her way down the aisle with her carry-on, she takes note of this fact, though today it seems extremely unimportant. And she does have a window seat.

Everyone on the plane is in a festive mood. People smile a

lot, though many faces show considerable fatigue, the ravages of a long and anxious night. But an almost manic mood prevails: the airport is clear, we're going home, the city has more or less survived. To all of which Lila adds to herself, and Karen is going back East, probably.

Everyone is seated, buckled in. The pilot's voice is telling the flight attendants to prepare for departure. The engines start their roar; they roar and roar. And nothing happens.

This goes on for some time—ten minutes, fifteen—until the engines are turned off, and they are simply sitting there on the runway, in the October Canadian sunlight. But the atmosphere on the plane is less impatient than might be imagined; it is felt that at least they are on their way. There may even be a certain (unacknowledged, unconscious) relief at the delay: San Francisco and whatever lies ahead do not have to be faced quite so soon.

The pilot announces a small mechanical glitch, which will be taken care of right away. And, perhaps twenty minutes later, the engines start again. And they are off, almost: the plane starts down the runway, gathering speed, and then, quite suddenly, it slows, and stops.

Jesus Christ. Now really. What now? We'll never. What in hell is going on? These sentiments echo around the cabin, where patience has worn audibly thin, until, apparently starting at the front row, where a smiling stewardess is standing, the rumor spreads: a dog has somehow got loose on the field; it will be a minute more. They have already been cleared for takeoff.

And then, with a motion that seems to be decisive, the plane moves forward, again. Glancing from her window, quite suddenly Lila sees—indeed!—a dog, running in the opposite direction, running back to Toronto. A large, lean, yellowish dog, whose gallop is purposeful, determined. He will get back to his place, but in the meantime he enjoys the run, the freedom of the forbidden field. His long nose swings up and down, his tail streams backward, a pennant, as Lila—watching from her window, headed at last back to San Francisco (probably)—begins in a quiet, controlled, and private way to laugh. "It was just so funny," she will say to Julian, later. "The final thing, that dog. And he looked so proud! As though instead of getting in our way he had come to our rescue."